Crimped to Death

A Divorced Diva Mystery

Tonya Kappes

Dedications

To the men in my life: Eddy, Austin, Brady, and Jack! They encourage and support me unconditionally.

To my readers! You keep me going and continue to help me live my dream. Thank you!

Chapter One

Honk, honk. Willow squeaked and rolled her ball around. *Honk.*

"The Beaded Dragonfly," I answered the old rotary-dial phone that hung on the wall in my bead shop.

I still smiled every single time I said my business name. It was mine, all mine.

"Yes. I understand," I said into the phone and looked out the big front window of the shop.

The light pink awning that hung over the storefront doors with The Beaded Dragonfly printed in black flapped in the morning breeze. The dragonfly mascot with the beaded tail was printed on the windows. The sun hit the tail of the dragonfly and projected the colors on the wall of the shop like a rainbow. It was truly magical. Exactly everything I had always dreamed of.

Honk, honk, honk. Willow batted the ball with her nose better than soccer players used their feet.

I tried not to laugh at how cute my pet pig was. "Your daughter's wedding jewelry will be just as beautiful as Margaret McGee's."

The day was turning out to be a beautiful day and the beads glistened throughout the store showing all of their brilliance. The large windows were big assets. I knew the natural light that shone through would give each bead and gem the sparkle that would set my bead shop apart from any other.

The front door flew open; just like a tornado Marlene Dietrich flew in for her afternoon shift at The Beaded Dragonfly, my lapidary.

Weak, weak, weak. Willow's tail twirled and she darted into the storage room in the back of the shop as fast as her little hooves could carry her.

As soon as she saw Marlene and her sky-high heels take the first step onto the hardwood floor, she was out of there.

"You better run." Marlene cackled and held her foot in the air, heel jabbing toward Willow. "I love pork on a stick, it's called a corn dog!"

Marlene's foot dropped and in one swift kick, she sent Willow's ball into *The Under*.

Sigh. I let out a long, deep breath. *The Under.*

To most people *The Under* of things probably didn't bother them. Me, well. . .I'm a different story. Even as a child I never liked *The Under*. *The Under* of beds, *The Under* of cars, even basements in houses were *Unders*. I had never explored the true reasons why I had never liked *The Under*, but I would think it would have to do with all the scariness of a monster *Under* the bed theory you heard about as a child.

Regardless, I never stuck my hand in *The Under* unless I had a big light illuminating the entire dark space.

"No. Not just as beautiful. Even better than Margaret McGee's jewelry." I gave Marlene the stink eye as she sashayed her long-legged, leopard-print wearing, hip-hugging, skin-tight jeggings legs toward me. "Great. I will mark you down. See you then."

I placed the phone back in it's cradle and grabbed the calendar next to the cash register laying on the glass counter and marked the new appointment with a mother of the bride.

"Really, Marlene? Must you always come in here and torment Willow?" I asked and put the calendar back.

"She's the one who started it." Marlene slid off her long leather gloves one finger at a time and dropped them on the counter.

Marlene didn't give scaring poor Willow a second thought. She unbuttoned her coat and hung it on the coat tree at the front of the shop near the door.

"Besides, you really shouldn't bring your pet to work." Marlene cocked her perfectly waxed brow and tugged on the v-neck part of her black top, tucking her girls away for the day.

I ignored her and looked at the list of clients I had on the schedule.

Marlene leaned on the counter and drummed her long red acrylic fingernails on the glass.

"Whatcha doing?" She batted her long, fake, implanted eyelashes.

"Working." I looked at her, a little irked by her cool manner. I pointed to the stack of boxes in the corner of the room that was filled with merchandise that needed to be placed on display. "Something you should be doing."

Marlene Dietrich had been working for me every since she stepped high-heeled into Swanee, Kentucky and she knew exactly what her job duties were. Unpack new inventory, put new inventory on the shelves, and answer the phone. Easy.

She and Willow were enemies from the start. Willow was scared of Marlene's boisterous cackle, not to mention the spikes on her shoes. Marlene loved to aggravate my poor pig.

"Did you have enough coffee this morning?" Marlene chomped on her gum. I could smell it and almost taste it.

"Because I can run down to Second Cup and get you one. Plus I have to drop off a new batch of Agnes's fudge."

"No I don't need a cup of coffee." I glanced up and glared at her. "I need you to unpack those boxes." I pointed over to the three stacked boxes in the far corner of the store.

"Fine." She dragged her hot pink purse toward her and took out a small plastic container filled with fudge. She took her gum out and stuck it right on top of the cash register. She took a piece of Agnes Pearl's delicious chocolaty treat out of the container and took a big bite. Her eyes closed. "Mmm." Her eyes opened. "You sure you don't want a piece?"

"Marlene, Food Watchers would call you a saboteur." I pushed the container away.

The smell alone would make me gain five pounds and tonight was my weigh-in night.

"Okay." She put the container back in her purse and pushed it toward me to stick it behind the counter. Her long nails plucked the wad of gum off the cash register and plopped it back in her mouth.

My eyes lowered and my nose curled as I watched middle-aged Marlene strut her thin body over to the boxes. I had to admit I was jealous.

I looked down into the glass counter. My dull brown hair fell into my face and I tucked a falling strand behind my ear. It wasn't a secret that after my divorce from *what's his name*, I had put on a few pounds and clothes with elastic waistbands had become my best friend.

A few months ago I decided to make a change and join Food Watchers. I had been really watching my weight and lost a few pounds, but not enough to really make a difference. Yet.

"Oh, these are beautiful." Marlene dangled a strand of coral beads in the air.

The sunlight gushed through the front windows, and hit the gems perfectly as the prisms bounced off the ceiling and walls.

“I can put these on my new necklace.” The words of excitement oozed out of her mouth like honey.

One good thing about Marlene, she showed up to work and she loved to design jewelry, which was altogether a plus for me.

“Oh no you won’t,” I assured her. “Those are for the new bridal line.”

She snarled and stuck them where they were supposed to go, the new bridal side of the shop. The right side of the lapidary was big enough for me to have a small café table with two chairs and a display case for unique and expensive beads a bride would wear on her wedding day.

I used that side of the shop for bridal consults and the other side of the shop for beading classes for customers, as well as the pre-made jewelry selection for anyone who wanted to buy, not make.

“The Divas would love them.” Marlene took one last look at the coral beads before she reluctantly dangled them on the hook that was meant just for them.

“I’m sure they would, but I have to make a living,” I reminded her.

The Divorced Divas, the Divas, for short, was a group formed in the most unlikely of ways. I was driving through Swanee during a rough day. Sean, my ex—aka what’s his name—hadn’t paid the alimony, and in the back of my head, I knew I needed to make a payment to the Sloans for rent.

The church sign read, “If you are divorced. Stop here. Meeting at 7pm.” As luck would have it, it was seven p.m. I whipped my little VW Beetle into the parking lot and marched right in.

The women greeted me with open arms, and we’ve been close ever since.

We found laughter and tears while bashing our ex-husbands and cheering each other on. Diva Flora White tended to take suggestions literally. Once, she cut all the armpits out of her ex-husband Bennie’s, shirts, put them in a garbage bag and dumped canned kidney beans on them. When he came to get his garbage bags of expensive lawyer clothes, he had a little treat inside. Needless to say, the Divas group got a visit from Noah Druck, our local cop. He suggested we bash our ex-husbands only figuratively from then on, unless we wanted a slew of lawsuits.

We Divas loved meeting and came up with all sorts of fun evil plots to hurt our exes in our heads, but that's where they stayed. The church wasn't able to accommodate additional meeting times, so we moved them to different Divas' houses, a hotel I had rented on the edge of town, and then finally to The Beaded Dragonfly.

"Good afternoon." Donovan Scott strolled through the door with two cups of welcomed coffee in his hands. "I thought you might need one of these."

He stood there, devilishly handsome with a nice smile on his face. His dimples deepened, making his blue eyes stick out even more against his olive skin.

"You were right." My heart sank into my stomach. "I do need an afternoon pick-me-up to get through the rest of the day."

I tugged my shirt down below my waist and walked from behind the counter. I couldn't hide my body behind it forever. Since I had been going to Food Watchers, I started taking daily walks with Diva Bernadine Frisk, plus I had also been taking a self-defense class from Donovan—as well as a going on a couple of dates with him.

The word date was used loosely. Most of the time it was late night conversations at his house. We had yet to take our relationship to anything more than kissing. Though it wasn't far from my mind. After all, I was a woman in need.

"That was a big hike yesterday." He walked toward me with the cup held out in front of him. His fingers touched mine, sending a zinging shock through my core. "I'm glad we decided to venture out."

Ahem. Marlene cleared her throat.

I had totally forgotten she was there. That was one thing Donovan did to me. . .made me forget my surroundings and drop the world from around me. That was a good sign. Something a man hadn't done for me in a long time.

"Marlene, you know Donovan." I gestured between the two. "Don't you have some fudge to deliver to Second Cup? I bet Bernadine is waiting for it."

Diva Bernadine was also my neighbor; she lived in a huge cabin across the lake from my little cottage—that was why it made it so easy for me to have a daily walk. She and I both did Food Watchers and kept each other accountable.

Recently she opened up a coffee shop in the middle of town, Second Cup, after she and Henry, her ex-ass, went to court for a fifth time. She realized she couldn't rely on him, so she's putting her alimony money to good use and investing in her future with the only café in town. Unfortunately, Henry moved back to Swanee and not only opened up a dental office, decided to sue Bernadine for a sixth time. This time he was suing to stop all alimony payments.

You could only imagine what all the Divas had planned for him.

"I guess I will do this later." Marlene left the boxes where she found them and went behind the counter to get her purse. "I'll be back." She gave Donovan the stare down as she passed us on her way out.

Marlene wasn't a big fan of Donovan. She adored my ex-ass. Only because he flashed his playboy smile and complimented her whenever he saw her, sending her body into full-on shivers.

Technically, Marlene was an honorary Diva. She loved to date the wealthy men that were on their way to the home of the near death, i.e. nursing homes. She enjoyed the lavish lifestyles they could give her, which didn't include marriage. Marlene definitely saw marriage as a ball and chain.

Unfortunately, her love 'em and leave 'em attitude came to an abrupt halt when she crossed the wrong ex-wife a few months ago. She's been on a man dry spell for a

while, making her cranky. I'd give her a few more months and she'll be back to her old self.

"Thank you so much." A half smile crossed my face as I watched her leave the shop.

I turned to Donovan. His gaze met mine and made my heart flutter. He grinned and straightened his shoulders.

"You look great." He pulled a chair out from under one the six tables where I host beading classes.

"Thank you." I felt my cheeks redden. I looked away.

Nervously, I picked at the edges of the coffee cup sleeve. We weren't used to being out in the public. It wasn't his doing. It was mine and I couldn't figure out why. Sean knew I was going on dates with Donovan, but I had never been on any dates other than with Sean. I did a lot of self talk about how it was just not a routine and I needed to go with the flow. Only the flow was always going against me.

Willow poked her head out of the storage room. When she saw Donovan, she ran out squealing with her tail twirling like a helicopter propeller. She loved Donovan and I was quickly thinking I did too.

Donovan bent down and gave her a good piggy pat, sending her into grunts and groans that only sounded right coming from a pig. He got up and walked over to the table.

"What do you have going on today?" Donovan sat down next to me and Willow plopped her big piggy booty on the floor and leaned up against Donovan.

He scooted the metal chair closer to me and rested his arm on the back of my chair. Being this close to him made me a little dizzy and I tried to throttle that feeling by talking aimlessly. Willow scooted with him.

"I have brides to talk to and beads to polish." I lifted the cup to my mouth and took a sip. I used my free hand to rub Willow's head. "These brides are crazy."

After Margaret McGee—Swanee's closest thing to a royal daughter with her perfectly put together mom and Bear McGee, the county attorney as a father—hired The Beaded Dragonfly to design her wedding jewelry for her and her bridesmaids, my business took off.

Brides from all around Swanee were hiring me with no expense spared to do their weddings and one up Margaret.

"You're right." I took another sip of the coffee. "This does hit the spot."

"I couldn't resist." He leaned in and his lips slowly descended to meet mine for a nice soft kiss. "I was on my way to my afternoon class and decided you just might need an afternoon pick-me-up."

Not only was Donovan a buff and hot self-defense instructor, he was also a computer professor at the local community college. Muscles and brains were a lethal combination for me.

"The coffee or the kiss?" I joked about which one might be the pick-me-up he was talking about.

"Both." He put his hands on my shoulders and gave me a little massage.

"That feels good." I shrugged my shoulders to my ears. "I had no idea how sore I was going to be from yesterday's hike. I thought I was in better shape since I had been walking with Bernadine."

Donovan and I had gone on our third date last night. We did a hike through the wooded area of Swanee, up and around the lake near my house. Bernadine and I had been in a habit of walking the lake shoreline, but Donovan had me hiking the woods.

"Will you be at the self-defense class tonight?" he asked.

This was Donovan's way of finding out if I was going to be available after the class. We hadn't really committed to exclusively dating each other, but I could feel it coming. He was a little older than me, way more mature than I was and I liked that about him.

"I have Margaret McGee's Wine and Bead class tonight and you never know how long that is going to take." I took another sip.

Though I would much rather spend time with him, I had a business to run.

Wine and Bead class had become a very popular class. I served wine for the four weekly classes while the participants made a couple pieces of jewelry. It was a great class for friends and family to take. Margaret McGee was hosting her own Wine and Bead class for her seven bridesmaids. She said that they have all been busy and she wanted them to stay in touch, so she paid for a full class session for just her group.

This meant I had two Wine and Bead classes each week for the next four weeks. Tonight was the start of Margaret's class.

"Maybe I should have given you a shot of Bailey's in that coffee." Donovan laughed, the lines around his eyes deepened as his smile widened. He got up. "I better go."

I stood up and Willow jumped to her hooves. She stared at us. Donovan reached out and pulled me to him. There was no denying the electricity bouncing off his chest into my heart.

"Thank you." I put my arms around him and looked up into his eyes. His dimples deepened and my heart beat faster.

The mere touch of his hand sent a warming shiver through me. He pulled me into a snug hug against his body. My head fit perfectly against his chest.

Ding. The bell over the shop rang out.

"Isn't this cute?" Sean Harper, my ex-ass, stood in the doorway with the antique chandelier I had wanted from our divorce to hang up in the shop.

Sean's grandmother had given him the most beautiful chandelier. A real chandelier; not just any old light. It was adorned with the most beautiful crystal beads in all shades of pink and red. I had no clue about its monetary value. I just knew that I loved it because of its beading elements.

Weak, weak, weak. Willow darted back and forth between Donovan and Sean. She loved them both and was confused on whom she wanted to be pet by. I completely understood how she felt.

"Sean." Donovan let me go and gave *what's his name* a man nod. He looked at me. His eyes were cold and proud. "Holly, I'll call you later."

"Okay." I smiled and waved him off.

Unsure of what to do in the situation, I grabbed my coffee off the table and walked back over to the counter.

Sean stepped aside and bent down to pat Willow—letting Donovan walk out. Donovan didn't turn back around and Sean's eyes didn't leave mine nor did his hands leave Willow.

"Really, Hol?" Sean asked using the name he had given me when we were married.

"You don't have the right to call me Hol anymore." It got my goat every time he shortened my name. "Holly. My name is Holly."

"Holly Harper." His playboy grin crossed his lips. "Don't forget that you still have *my* name."

"Trust me." I glared at him. "If it wasn't a hassle to change it and all the documents in my name for the shop, I would have gotten rid of Harper a long time ago."

Groink, groink, groink. Willow stopped shy of the storage room door and looked back. She hated when Sean and I fought. She was just like a little kid. Our little kid.

"It's okay, girl." He put the chandelier on one of the tables and bent down, calling her over.

"I'm so glad one of my girls is glad to see me." He didn't bother to look up to see my reaction.

Willow plopped down with her legs sprawled out and then flipped on her back. She loved a good belly scratch.

"We aren't your girls anymore." I patted my leg for Willow to get up. "Remember? You changed all of that when you realized you didn't want us."

I still never knew what had happened between us. I thought we were happy and my weight proved it. He hated the fact I was wearing elastic-waistband pants and I hated he spent all his time drinking with his buddies at The Livin' End.

"I've changed." He picked up the chandelier off the floor and walked over to the counter. He pointed to the spot above the cash register. "Here?"

"Yes." I couldn't wait to see the beautiful light installed in the shop.

If it weren't for me saving Sean's ass. . .again, I would have never gotten my hands on the chandelier. I guess you could say it was my payment for saving his life. Literally.

"I'm going to get some tools from my truck." He walked to the door and turned back to look at me.

The gaze was a little too long. I looked away and grabbed the schedule, pretending to work. I didn't know whom I was kidding. When Sean was around, it was hard for me to concentrate on anything other than my fingers going around his neck. He might have left me, but my heart hadn't fully left him, even though I was trying to move on with Donovan.

Sean was the only handyman around town. He owned Sean's Little Shack Handyman Service. I hated to admit it, but he was good at what he did. And all the Divas used him. He had them eating out of his hand.

Within seconds he was back in the shop with all sorts of tools to install the chandelier.

"So are you dating the teacher?" Sean had grabbed the ladder from the storage room and shimmied up it.

"We've gone on a couple of dates." I pretended not to pay him any attention. "Not that it's any of your business."

I grabbed a silver cloth and worked my way down the silver findings. They needed to be polished and it was a mindless activity.

"What do you see in him?" Sean asked before a rush of girls came in the shop. His green eyes pierced me.

The bell dinged, giving me the perfect excuse to look away from him.

"Hi girls." I greeted them and took note of the time.

They waved and made their way around the shop oohing and awing over the shiny beads.

Most of the high school girls came in to see what I had put on sale or what my latest creation was. They were perfect advertisements for me. Plus they let me in on all the latest beading designs.

Every once in a while I would glance over at Sean. He wasn't dressed in his usual handyman overalls that he insisted he wear while working. He was in a pair of light colored jeans and a black plaid long-sleeved shirt with the sleeves rolled up perfectly on his toned forearms.

His shaggy blond hair was perfect next to his tanned face. His jaw set tense as he concentrated on not getting electrocuted.

Girls, girls, girls. Sean's phone sang out from the cell phone clip that was pinned on his belt.

"You still have Mötley Crüe as your ringtone?" I rolled my eyes.

The girls giggled from the other side of the room. They pointed and stared at Sean. He was hot.

"Sean's Little Shack," he answered and got down from the ladder.

While he put the ladder back into the storage room, I tried to listen to what he was saying, but couldn't make it out.

"I'm back." Marlene strutted back into the shop. "Bernadine said she'd just meet you at the fat meeting."

"Seriously?" I asked Marlene. "Don't you have a filter?"

"What?" She shrugged. "I call it what it is."

I shook my head. It was almost time for my weekly Food Watchers meeting and weigh-in. I was starving and I hoped the scales showed it.

"Hey, handsome." Marlene squealed when Sean came out of the storage room. "I didn't know you were here or I would have come back sooner." She winked, chomped her gum, and ran her finger down his arm. He blushed. "If you need a date to the Barn Dance, let me know." She winked and blew him an air kiss.

"I don't think I could handle a woman like you," Sean's southern drawl was reeling Marlene right on in.

"I'll be gentle," she teased and looked at me. "What?" she asked when she saw I was not amused. "Holly Harper, how can you not look at those eyes and be drawn back in? You were one lucky girl."

"He was one lucky guy." I directed her to the stacked boxes.

"Slave driver." She wiggled her way back over to the unfinished boxes.

She did make me wonder whom Sean would take to the annual Barn Dance. He never missed it and was never alone.

Chapter Two

"I'm going to kill Henry Frisk!" Bernadine stomped her feet as we waited in line to be weighed at our weekly Food Watchers meeting. Her jade eyes narrowed, and she folded her arms across her chest. The velour green jumpsuit looked good against her long red hair. She huffed, "I honestly can't believe he moved back here." She held a piece of paper in her hand. "And if he thinks I'm going to pay for some interior decorator bill that costs as much as my monthly alimony, he's crazy!"

Bernadine had to be the neatest person in Swanee, right down to her appearance. Bernadine and Henry's marriage was like the ones you hear about where the couple wakes up one day and realize that they don't know each other.

He'd come out better off than Bernadine. She got the house on the lake across from my cottage, and he got their huge mansion in Ft. Myers, Florida. There was still a bitter taste in Bernadine's mouth. After all, she had moved to Swanee for him.

Henry thought he wanted the small town life, while she wanted the beach and sand. When it came down to the end, Bernadine was the one who ended up loving Swanee and all her new friends.

I extended my arm with my key fob pointed toward my car and clicked it to make sure the doors were locked. I had parked next to the cutest yellow Fiat with new tags.

Bernadine handed me the piece of crinkled paper.

"This is an almost eight thousand dollar bill," I said, clearly surprised by the number.

I was stunned at first because she said that was about as much as she had gotten in alimony, but I knew she was kidding. There was no way she was getting that much alimony. *Was she*? "He wants you to pay this?"

"Yes. I've never even heard of this place. Buskins Interiors." The lines between her brows creased. She ran her finger between her eyes. "I need to use the money for these stress lines he's giving me."

"I can help you right here." Charlie St. Clair, the Food Watchers Specialist, oozed with enthusiasm that pretty much made me nauseous. "You look great Bernadine."

Of course she was all happy and chipper with her spirit hands, big boobs, five-foot-seven-inch thin frame, and to make it worse, perfect cheekbones.

I rolled my eyes and looked into the meeting room while Charlie buttered up little butterball Bernadine. In fact, I thought Bernadine looked like she had gained a few pounds. But like a tick-a-lock, I kept my mouth shut.

The meeting was located in one big room with ten rows of yellow chairs. There were three workstations with computers and floor scales along with a Food Watchers Specialist in matching yellow shirts and khaki pants.

I looked awful in yellow, but not *Charlie*. I bet she looked good in everything.

"Anyway," Bernadine peeled off the *My Name Is* sticker and stuck it right on her boob. She sat in Charlie's chair and tied her running shoes back up.

Charlie cocked her perfectly sculpted brows, twitched her lips and held her hand out for me to give her my weigh-in log.

"Well?" The enthusiasm she had for Bernadine wasn't oozing for me. She smacked the name sticker on the counter for me to fill out. "I have a full line of people waiting. Are you weighing or not?"

My mouth opened, then I snapped it shut in fear I would start a war of words. I decided my best revenge would be to lose more weight and look better than her. I took my shoes off because every single ounce counted when on the scale.

"He wants to take me back to court to stop the alimony because I opened Second Cup." Bernadine slipped her bangle bracelets on her wrist. "It's bad enough he moved back here, but to take me back to court."

I slapped my weigh-in chart on the counter for Charlie to gawk at. Charlie tapped on her computer keyboard and didn't pay any attention to me like she did Bernadine.

"Step up," Charlie said in a monotone voice.

"And to think that he sold that Ft. Myers house for over two million dollars. He doesn't need the piddly money he gives me each month." Bernadine brushed her hair behind her ears. "I told Flora to call in her favor that her ex-ass owes her because I was going to hire him as my lawyer."

"That is a great idea," I said and stepped up on the scale.

I held my breath wondering if air weighed anything.

"Get off." Charlie tapped on the computer before she wrote on my paper. "Down a pound."

"Yay!" Bernadine hopped off the chair. "I think I found it." She winked and patted her belly. "I guess the smells from the café are making me gain. I swear I haven't ventured from my healthy eating."

Bernadine had a perplexed look on her face like she was contemplating what she had said. She pulled a Ziploc baggie full of carrots and celery out of the zippered pocket of her jumpsuit jacket. She always carried a Ziploc baggie full of some sort of veggies. And somehow Willow always ate them, leaving little for Bernadine.

"Oh, Bernadine." Charlie's happy chirp was back. She pulled a little brown wrapper from underneath the counter. "Here is Barbie's latest fat-free dessert. We hope you decide to carry it in Second Cup."

Excitement twirled in my stomach, or maybe it was starvation twirling, but I couldn't wait to get my sample of Barbie's new treat.

Barbie was one of those icons who had the one name like Madonna, Beyoncé, Cher. Barbie.

She was Ms. Food Watchers herself. She owned and operated Food Watchers. Lately she had ventured out into decadent desserts and gave samples out to the attendees. There was a display of them in the lobby of Food Watchers and Bernadine had started featuring a few in her shop.

I stood there waiting eagerly for my sample. Bernadine popped hers in her mouth.

"Delicious." Bernadine closed her eyes and chewed slowly. My mouth watered. She licked her fingers.

"I'm sorry," Charlie said apologetically and I actually thought she meant it. "I'm all out."

"No problem." I waved it off and followed Bernadine into the meeting room up to the front row like we did every week.

Me, I'd stay way in the back. Last seat in fact. But not Bernadine. She likes to be front and center. *Everywhere.*

"Why am I gaining weight?" Bernadine wiggled her fingers and winked hello to a few other members.

"It's only a pound." I sat down and waited for the big show to start. "We can walk that off."

"If you find time away from *Donovan Scott."* Bernadine winked right before the lights dimmed and the disco ball in the center of the meeting room was turned up to high.

The mirror ball swirled around. The reflection darted off the excited members' faces as they clapped, hooted and hollered in anticipation for Ms. Food Watchers to make her weekly appearance.

“Is everybody ready?” A loud voice boomed over the intercom.

Every single person had a big smile on their face, as if some Hollywood megastar had just walked into the room. Enthusiastically, we clapped to the beat of the music. A couple of people let out a few hoots, hollers, and double-finger whistles.

The clapping and swaying was infectious. Raucous music was blared and the mirror ball stopped to make room for the streaming spot light. They rotated in the center of the room.

My toes began to tap like they had a mind of their own. *Well, a little sway too and fro isn’t going to hurt anyone,* I thought. *When in Rome.*

The members in the center aisle parted as a tall, blond, gazelle-like Barbie made her way through the crowd. She held a microphone in one hand and greeted her eager, food-deprived acolytes with the other.

Ms. Food Watchers. Envy chilled through me as my eyes traveled up her legs to her cinched waist and ending at her big happy smile.

"Hello!" She sang out when she got to the front of the room and hopped up on the small stage right in front of Bernadine and me. "Is everyone ready to lose some weight this week?"

I had to shield my eyes from the glare of her pro-white dentals.

Bernadine nudged me. "She's going to Henry's practice now. Damn," she leaned a little closer to me, "he never got my teeth that white."

"I said," she repeated as if the yells and screams that rattled the place weren't loud enough, "Is everybody ready to lose some weight?" Barbie pumped her fists in the air and the crowd erupted in even louder cheers.

"I swear this is a cult," I leaned over and whispered in Bernadine's ear.

She probably didn't hear me. In true cult style, Bernadine's eyes were locked on Barbie as she cheered and fist pumped right along with the rest of them.

Chapter Three

On nights of beading classes, I closed the shop around a quarter to six. That way, it gave me time to move the tables a little closer together and get out bead-boards for each beader along with their own set of tools.

"1,2,3," I counted out the crimping tools from the shelf in the storage room. I needed twelve all together.

The crimp tool was the most important beading tool in my opinion. It was the instrument that squished the crimp bead or other findings to complete the beading project.

"I'm back," Marlene yelled from the front of the shop.

Marlene tended The Beaded Dragonfly while I went to my Food Watchers meeting. When I got back, she left to go get Agnes Pearl. Marlene lived with Agnes. Agnes hired Marlene before Marlene's high heel planted on the ground when she first came to Swanee.

Marlene needed a job and Agnes was looking for an "Agnes keeper", someone to keep her company, though Marlene did things like go to the grocery for Agnes and picked up around the house. Saying Marlene was cleaning Agnes's house was a stretch.

At a spry eighty-five years old, Agnes probably took care of Marlene instead of the other way around. Especially since she had that new eye surgery and she can see like a teenager with perfect vision.

"I'll be out in a minute." I grabbed a few more items like the Acu-flex beading wire.

I found it to be the most durable wire when making jewelry and I wanted to make sure I let Margaret and her friends use the best of the best for their Wine and Bead class. Margaret McGee spreading the word and wearing my designs was better than any paid advertising I could have ever done.

"I told her to go for more money." Agnes Pearl adjusted her turban. Today's choice was bright yellow with a green plastic emerald in the dead center. "He is a low-down dirty dog if you ask me." Agnes nodded and hugged Cheri as they exchanged the news about Bernadine's situation.

Nobody was asking her. But that was what you had to love about Agnes. She was old and like most old people, she spoke her mind.

Cheri lived in the apartment above The Beaded Dragonfly. She was a local college student who not only worked a few hours a week for me for extra money, but she loved Willow. Bless Cheri's heart, she was a savior. She took Willow for her daily walks while I was busy around the shop.

Cheri adjusted the beret on the top of her head. She was so pretty with her straight brown hair and blunt bangs.

Don't be cruel. Cheri's phone belted out. She looked at it. Her big brown eyes popped. "Oh, I gotta take this." She disappeared into the storage room.

Cheri was fun and young. She was the fly-by-your-seat Diva who had gotten married at the age of nineteen in a quickie wedding in Vegas by. . .you guessed it, an Elvis impersonator. The next day her annulment was just as quick, making her a Divorced Diva.

"What do you think about that jerk?" Agnes Pearl asked me. Her eyes narrowed.

Without asking her whom she was talking about, I knew. Henry Frisk. He was a jerk for showing up in Swanee after he hated it, suing Bernadine yet again, and taking business from Kevin Russell. Kevin had been the only dentist in Swanee for as long as I could remember. He never had to worry about competition. Until now.

"I heard Dr. Russell confronted him at the Barn Dance meeting last night about how Henry was stealing Dr. Russell's clients." Agnes picked at the wispy pieces of hair sticking out of her turban next to her ear.

"Did they really?" Flora's head was tilted to the side. Her cell phone was wedged between her ear and shoulder. "Hey, gotta go," she said to the recipient on the other end. She sat her designer handbag on the table and planted her butt in the chair next to Agnes. "Dish."

"You should know more than us." Marlene put small five-millimeter sterling silver round beads in small bowls for me. "Damn," she murmured when a couple bounced off the glass.

"Marlene!" I groaned as I watched them bounce right into *The Under*. "I hope you know that I'm putting cleaning The Under on your to-do list."

"Whatever." Marlene shrugged. She and I both knew she wasn't going to bend over, ass in the air, for stray beads. A man. . . maybe. . .beads. No.

The jingle bells rang over the shop door. Margaret and a couple of her bridesmaids came in.

"Hi girls." I waved them in. "Sit anywhere. I'm just getting all the wine and beads ready."

"So, this is what you do?" Charlie from Food Watchers walked in with the group.

"You two know each other?" Margaret's voice raised in excitement. "Holly Harper is the best jewelry designer ever," Margaret squealed and grabbed Charlie's hand

dragging her to an empty table next to the gossip sessions some of the Divas were having.

"Anyway, I was at Second Cup when Henry came in and told Bernadine that she was going to get a subpoena to go back to court. And. . ." Marlene looked around, she leaned over the table so Flora and Agnes could hear her. "He said something about a life insurance policy about to come due and he was glad she wasn't getting a damn dime."

"He said damn dime?" Agnes asked.

Marlene nodded.

"He's got more nerve than Carter's got liver pills." Agnes Pearl was steaming.

Agnes Pearl was not one to mess around with. She was the wealthiest widow in Swanee. She might be a couple cups of crazy, but she never messed around when it came to money.

"I told Flora she needed to call your ex." She pointed her long acrylic nails toward Flora.

"Marlene," I interrupted. "Can you help me with the refreshments?" I asked on the way to the storage room where I had to make room for Cheri and Willow.

"I'm going to take her for a quick walk." Cheri held Willow's leash in her hand.

Willow was so proud; she high-stepped out into the shop until she saw Marlene coming toward us.

Weak, weak, weak. She tried to dart into *The Under* of the closest shelf; her butt wouldn't fit no matter how hard she tried to wedge herself and besides the leash wasn't long enough.

"I've been craving ham all day! Get me the salt shaker." Marlene cackled before she disappeared in the back.

"Don't listen to mean old Marlene." Cheri bent down and patted Willow on the head before Willow scampered out the door as Bernadine came in.

With the wine almost gone and the energy level of the bead shop on acceleration, I announced that the class for

this week would be ending in about fifteen minutes, which was around nine p.m.

You would think three hours was plenty of time to string an entire jewelry set, but not with chatty Margaret and her group of friends. Along with her group of six and the six Divas, we had a full house.

The jingle bells chimed over the door.

"Sorry ladies," Sean apologized when he looked around the room. He held up one of the red gems that went with the chandelier he had wired and put up earlier in the shop. "I found this in my truck this afternoon and wanted to be sure to attach it." He flashed his million-dollar playboy smile. "It's a beauty, but not to its full potential if not all the pieces are there."

Ugh. And this was why I could never date him again. Sean never knew when to turn on the charm around other women, causing them to fall at his feet.

"Hi, Sean." Charlie stood up and held the beading wire by the end. The uncrimped side.

Ping, ping, ping. One-by-one all the beads that took her three hours to string hit the tile floor and found their way into the different *Unders.*

"No!" I scrambled to the floor as Willow made a mad dash out of the storage room to gobble up all the round gems. Cheri grabbed her. The beads were lost to *The Under*.

"There goes some profit." I threw my hands in the air and then stuck my hand out for Sean to give me the damn piece so he could get the hell out of here. "I'll attach it."

Granted, I probably wouldn't take the time to get the ladder and do it, but I wanted him out as quickly as possible. He was creating all kinds of havoc.

"I could never let you get up on a ladder, Hol." Sean quickly grabbed the ladder and was halfway up.

There wasn't much I could do but shoot darts at him out of my eyes and hope he'd fall off the ladder. Not hurting him of course, but a broken leg that would keep him away from me. Away from the female society. Was that too much to ask?

"Oops." Charlie playfully shrugged and walked over to the ladder. She held onto the ladder as he climbed up. "I can hold it steady."

He looked down, straight into her cleavage. He smiled. "Thanks, Charlie."

"I wondered when I was going to see you again." Charlie shuffled her feet, tucked a piece of her hair behind her ear and shrugged her shoulders toward him.

"Two hands." I gestured out in front of me like I was holding on to the ladder. Charlie was too busy flirting to even realize she didn't have one single finger on the ladder.

"How about tonight?" Sean ignored me, hung the gem on the light and did a little hop off the ladder.

Charlie giggled.

"We can knock back a few at The Livin' End." He took his phone out of his back pocket. "What's your address and phone number?"

My mouth dropped open. My eyes slid over to the Diva table. I thought Agnes Pearl's false teeth were going to come tumbling out. Cheri tapped Agnes's chin. Agnes's mouth shut just like a Venus Fly-trap. Marlene chomped her gum and stared at them. Cheri shook her head. Bernadine and Flora were busy elbowing each other.

Ahem. I cleared my throat and held the door open.

"Two can play this game," Sean whispered and referred to Donovan when he walked past me.

I slammed the door behind him causing all the shelves up against the walls to rattle.

"No!" I screamed as a few of the bins of beads tumbled to the ground and bounced around until they found their way into *The Under.*

"Don't worry." Marlene held her hands in the air. "I've got it."

Chapter Four

"1,2,3 4," I counted eleven crimp tools for the fifth time.

Sure I was a little discombobulated from Sean asking Charlie out right in front of me, but I knew how to count.

"Where is the twelfth crimping tool?" I looked under each chair and table looking for the blue rubber-handled tool. "It has to be here somewhere."

"I'd like to put it up Henry's you-know-what." Bernadine's brows lifted. Her neck reddened to the color of her hair.

"Goodnight," Margaret and her friends trickled out of the shop after they gave their bead boards with their unfinished projects to Cheri who would put them safely on a shelf in the storage room until the next Wine and Bead session with this group.

I continued to look around for the tool, but gave up once Cheri was done and we were packing up for the night.

"I hate to hear about your troubles." Cheri pulled a seat up next to Bernadine.

"Don't worry about it. I'm sure Bennie will be able to stick it to him." Bernadine's eyes slid over to Flora who was too busy talking on her phone to even hear what Bernadine had said. "If not," she gestured between the Divas, "we can take care of him."

Collectively, we all laughed, knowing how much fun we had plotting the demise of the ex-asses who hurt us.

Flora twitched her fingers in the air as she left the store. "Toodles," she called out.

"I wouldn't give that bastard an inch," Agnes gave Bernadine a cutting stare. "Not even an inkling of an inch."

"Don't you worry about that." Bernadine gave a delicate nod that said volumes. "I'll see that bastard dead before he even thinks he can get any part of Second Cup."

"Let's not talk about all of that." I shook my head clearing my thoughts of where the hell I put the crimp tool. "I say we head on down to The Livin' End to grab a beer."

"I'm ready for bed." Agnes did chin stretches, elongating her neck. "I have to do my neck exercises and get my beauty sleep. I'm still on the market for a new man."

"The only new man you are going to get, is one in the home of the near death." Marlene cackled. Agnes did not. "Just joking."

Marlene helped Agnes up, and before too long, they were out the door.

"And to think that we all thought that you were over him," Bernadine said.

I backed up and used the counter for support.

"I am over him." I bit the edge of my lip. "I bet that Charlie knew he was my ex and that was why she has been so nasty to me at Food Watchers."

"Nasty? I haven't seen her be anything but sweet." Bernadine leaned forward, propping her elbows up on the table. Her baggie tumbled out the pocket of her velour jacket.

Willow rushed out of the storage room. She was used to hearing the crackle of Bernadine's snack packs. Willow sat next to Bernadine's feet, nudging her calf with her snout. Without even giving it a second thought, Bernadine opened the baggie and took out two carrots. One for her and one for Willow.

"She never remembers my name. She always gives you the last treat they pass out," I said loudly over the crunch. "And she encourages you on your weight loss and never says a word to me."

"She does too talk to you." Bernadine was quick to come to Charlie's rescue.

"If you want to count her saying *step up* and *step down,* in her monotone voice. Fine." I shrugged hoping this conversation was taking the heat off me and my confused feelings about Charlie and Sean's date.

"Still, it has to hurt that your ex asked her out right in front of you." Cheri patted Willow on the butt.

Willow danced a little back jig, twirling her tail like a whip-a-whirl.

"I don't have feelings for him." I pointed to the chandelier. "I got what I wanted."

"You sure did. And now my ex-ass wants what I got." Bernadine brought it back full circle. "I do want a beer."

That was all it took for me to finish cleaning up the little snippets of wire, crimp beads, and glass beads from the Wine and Bead class. I figured I'd find the crimp tool later.

Cheri took Willow for a quick walk and got her snuggled in her bed in the storage room. I would stop by after a quick drink and get her.

Bernadine didn't lift a finger to help. All she did was cuss and fuss over Henry, which I didn't blame her. If it wasn't my own shop that needed to be cleaned, I probably wouldn't have raised a finger either.

When I first opened The Beaded Dragonfly, Sean alluded that he wanted a piece of it since I had to use his alimony to help make the payments, but I shot that down. Hell, his alimony payments were few and far between. When he did make them, they were never on time.

With the three of us wedged into my little VW Beetle, we drove through Swanee to the other end where The Livin' End sat on the edge of town. The parking lot was full which put me at ease a little. If Sean was in there with little Miss Prissy Pants, I would be able to hide in a dark booth.

The thought of him with the beanpole did piss me off. She was exactly the type Sean liked before we did get married and when I was a beanpole. I had already lost ten pounds, but had at least thirty more to go.

"Let's go." I got out of the car and immediately spotted Sean's handyman truck on the side of the building.

We scurried across the parking lot, each of us knowing what the other was thinking without saying it. But then Bernadine did.

"I'll back you." Bernadine did a double-fisted jab in the air. "Maybe I can take my frustrations out on someone."

I knew better. If Charlie said something to Bernadine, Bernadine would melt talking to her.

"I'll kick him square in the nuts." Cheri did a sidekick like the one Donovan had taught us in class.

"I don't care about Sean and Skinny Ass." I shrugged.

"You might not have feelings for him, but he shouldn't flaunt it in your face." Bernadine flung the door open.

The jukebox blared some slow country song. The drunks that were belly up to the bar sang along while holding their mugs in the air, swaying back and forth as if they were reliving some sort of fun past. Smoke like an early morning fog hung over the pool tables to the far left of the bar.

Cheri held her finger in the air, pointing over to an open bar-top table.

I mouthed "no", but it was too late. Bernadine had nearly knocked over everyone in her line of vision getting to the last table in the place. The only problem was that it was right in front of the dance floor.

The last thing I wanted to look at were happy couples slow dancing to Garth Brooks or Little Big Town. That didn't bother Bernadine or Cheri any. They toe-tapped their way into the chairs, not worried a bit about me. All that *I've got your back* crap had flown right out of their heads.

"This is a great seat," Cheri said and gave the bartender a little nod and held up three fingers.

That was the only thing you had to do to get a bottle of beer at The Livin' End. Within seconds, a cold brew was right in the palm of our hands.

I glanced around the bar and spotted Sean on the far end. Alone. Charlie wasn't anywhere to be seen. Maybe she did have some sense in her to not fool around with a no good sonofabitch like Sean Harper.

"Do you see them?" Bernadine asked.

"I see him." I nodded toward the end of the bar. "He's alone."

"See. He didn't follow through." Cheri clinked the top of her bottle to mine. "He probably didn't even call her."

"I wouldn't be so sure." Bernadine craned her thick neck around me. Her eyes seared toward the entrance. "And dressed to seduce."

In awe, the three of us stood there with our mouths wide open. Every single man in the bar stared and since almost everyone in the bar was a man, the entire place went silent, except for the jukebox. Her long flowing blond hair had been straightened and was as shiny as a new penny. She wore black leather pants so snug that no-way, no-how Sean Harper's hand was going to fit between her skin and the tight-fitting pants. The fitted white blouse was tucked in and contoured to every curve on her boobs and waist. The black push-up bra peek-a-boo'ed at the fourth unbuttoned button and her cleavage was as tight as bark on a tree. Silver chained jewelry dripped around her neck and was perfectly placed on the blouse. The bangles up her wrist were a far cry from the glass-beaded bracelet she was working on at The Beaded Dragonfly Wine and Bead class.

"Shit. I want to look like her." Bernadine picked up her beer and swigged it down. She nudged me. "Holly?"

It was like a trance. An old slow motion movie. Sean stood up. His eyes locked with Charlie's. Both had big grins on their faces. She wrapped her skinny, long fingers around his neck, bringing him closer, and whispered something funny in his ear because Sean belted out in laughter, tossing his shaggy hair to the side. The two of them sat down. She didn't order a beer like the rest of us. She ordered a martini.

"Who orders martinis at The Livin' End?" I asked in disgust and turned back around.

"Her," Cheri snarled.

We all hunched over the table in silence having one round after the other. After a few rounds, my eyeballs began to float. I excused myself and made my way back up front to where the bathrooms were located.

"Excuse me." I was too busy looking down, feeling sorry for myself when I ran smack dab into Noah Druck.

"Noah!" I held my hand up to my heart. "You nearly gave me a heart attack."

I moved my way around him, but he stepped right back in front of me. His hand rested on his gun that was snapped into his holster buckled around his waist. The lines between his blue eyes creased. He took a deep breath.

"Have you had one too many, Holly?" he asked with conviction in his voice.

"I'm not breaking a law. I have to pee, so if you will excuse me." I walked around to his other side and he stepped in front of me again. "Noah Druck, I will not dance with you tonight." I laughed and barreled my way around him.

It was a shame Noah was a bull-headed cop. He was cute and Sean's old best friend. If I was to go out with Noah, that would really get Sean's goat. It wasn't that I was still in love with Sean, I was still angry with Sean for leaving me. Any revenge sounded good. Especially right now with a little liquid courage in me.

All three stalls in the bathroom were taken. My toe tapped waiting, holding back the pee-pee feeling. The sound of a flush made me happy to know I was next.

"Well, well. I had no idea you were married to Sean Harper." Charlie stepped out of the stall.

Without giving her the time of day, I darted in the stall and locked it. I glanced at the toilet. Charlie probably peed sprinkles of gold. Or angels sang when she urinated.

The other two people in the other stalls flushed. I took my time so I didn't have to face Charlie at the sink, but my plan failed. She stood looking at herself in the mirror. She got her lipstick out of her clutch and slowly rolled it up. Red.

"I can't believe you ever let a man like Sean go." She talked and glided the matte finish across and around her lips before she pressed them together. She quickly took a picture of herself with her cell phone. "Hashtag selfie. Hashtag best date ever."

I clicked the soap dispenser at the sink and nothing came out. In order to get soap, I had to use the one in front of her.

"Excuse me." I butted my way over.

"You know." She had her hand on her hip as she cocked her leg out and leaned forward. She whispered, "If you think that going to Food Watchers will get you to look like me and win Sean back, you're crazier than I thought."

"Over my dead body!" I screamed out of anger. "I'll show you crazy!"

Well I screamed it after she pranced out of the bathroom. I gripped the edge of the sink. I was about to be sick to my stomach when a stall door opened.

"Excuse me," the woman said, her back pressed up against the stall doors. She wiggled her way past me with fear in her eyes.

"Oh Carol." I greeted Dr. Russell's receptionist. She stood about six feet tall, a platinum blonde with a snow-white complexion. She wore black leather pants and a fringed leather vest over a white tee shirt. She had a biker boyfriend who was always playing pool. "I didn't mean what I said." Nervously I laughed. "Too many beers."

"Don't worry about it, Holly." She stopped shy of the door. "Isn't it about time you come in for a cleaning?"

Fear oozed throughout my body. I had never been fond of going to the dentist and it took everything in my soul to not only make an appointment, much less go to the appointment.

"Probably." I smiled, with my mouth shut. "I'll call you tomorrow," I said with no intention what so ever to call.

"Okay. Great." Carol opened the door and turned back around. "Holly, you are much prettier than that girl. Trust me. I know."

I ran my finger along the elastic of my jeans. I was going to show Miss Prissy Pants that I didn't need the encouragement she gave Bernadine or the low-fat delicious-looking treats to help me make my goal. I didn't want Sean. But, there wasn't anything wrong with me wanting *Sean* to desperately want *me* back.

The slow song pulled all the couples out on the dance floor, including Charlie and Sean. Noah had made himself comfortable on my stool. At least it looked that way until I got a little closer.

"What's wrong?" I put my hand on Bernadine's back when I noticed tears dripping down her cheeks.

"Henry is dead." Bernadine's eyes dipped down. "I can't believe it."

My eyes slid to Noah. He pinched his lips together and nodded.

"Noah said he was stabbed." Bernadine heaved up and down. "I think I would like to go."

"Yes." I agreed.

"Where were you tonight?" Noah pulled out his little notebook from the front pocket of his police uniform.

"Why are you asking me this?" An uneasy feeling dipped into my gut, putting a knot in my throat. I swallowed.

"There was some sort of beading tool left at the scene." Noah rolled his eyes. "I have to check out every detail at the crime scene."

"You know what a beading tool looks like?" My eyes narrowed.

"No, but Officer Kiss pointed it out and apparently she's an avid beading person." Noah had no idea what he was talking about.

"Officer Kiss has had it out for The Divas every since we found her best friend with Flora's husband." I reminded him about the time he had made his first little visit to our church divorced group.

Granted Officer Kiss's best friend was gay and that was how Bennie came out. Bennie did work for the Swanee police and he paid Officer Kiss a visit about a case. Officer Kiss had her friend over and introduced the two. It was all down hill from there for Flora. She ended up bitter and single. Bennie ended up a successful lawyer with a lover.

This prompted Diva Flora's armpit-kidney-bean-garbage-bag incident and Noah's subsequent visit to our meeting to give us the advice to bash the ex-asses in word only, unless we wanted to face more visits from him. So we decided to move our little group of six to The Beaded Dragonfly once it was open for business.

We all knew that Officer Beverly Kiss was the one who told Noah to visit with us because it would look funny if she was there on behalf of her friend and Bennie, not on official police business.

"Holly, I have to turn over every leaf." Noah's eyes lowered. A shadow from his lashes lined the top of his cheek. "I know you gals are scorned from your divorces and you know what they say about a woman scorned."

"Yeah." Cheri reached over and cupped Bernadine's shaking hands. "A woman scorned does better research than an FBI agent. Let's go."

Cheri jumped up and pulled on her moto jacket.

"The Divas joked about killing our exes, but we never wanted any of them seriously hurt. At least not dead." I stood up to help Bernadine to her feet.

"Damn, Sean is moving up in the world." Noah nodded toward the *happy* couple just as they twirled in front of us. "Anyway Holly, I'll be by the shop tomorrow to check out your inventory."

"Am I a suspect or something?" I scowled.

Noah shrugged.

"That's it." I grabbed Bernadine by the arm because she wasn't moving. She had to be in shock. The heat in my throat dampened my armpits. Blood pressure rose. Had Noah Druck lost his mind? "I've seen enough and I've had enough. Let's go."

Hearing that Noah could possibly think I could be a potential suspect for Bernadine's ex-ass and watching every man swoon over Charlie dug a hole in my stomach, making me hungry. Not for food. For Donovan.

Chapter Five

"Are you home?" Immediately I called Donovan after I dropped Cheri off at The Beaded Dragonfly and grabbed Willow.

"Of course I'm home." Donovan sounded a little drowsy. "It's two a.m. Are you okay?"

"I'm fine." It felt good to hear someone ask about my well-being. "Bernadine's husband was found stabbed to death and I just got her in bed after giving her a sleeping pill."

"Gosh, Holly." I could hear the sympathy in his voice. It was exactly what I needed. "I'm so sorry. Do you want to come over?"

"I have Willow." I always felt it was necessary to warn people when I had the little dust-bunny-eating piggy with me.

"She's always welcome." Donovan didn't leave me any room to rebut. "I'm going to open the door and turn on the porch light."

That was the thing I loved about Donovan. A few months ago after Doug Sloan, brother of my best friend Ginger, was found dead on the floor of my bead shop, I signed up for the self-defense classes taught by Donovan and that was how we met.

When the noose got tighter around my neck during the investigation, Donovan showed me how to use computer equipment to help find the real killer and he insisted I stay at his house for safety.

Of course nothing happened but a few kisses and snuggles, but I was hoping that was going to change.

Donovan's landscape at his house was immaculate. The hedges were neatly trimmed, and the edging along the sidewalk was perfect. Even the colors in the flowerbed were coordinated. The stars twinkled over them, sending little pops of color into the dark night sky.

He waved from the front door. His tall slender frame brought a smile to my face. It was good to see a friendly smile, especially in the middle of the night.

"Let's go." I got out of the Beetle and tugged on Willow's leash for her to come to my side.

Groink, groink. Willow waddled over the console. I picked her up and put her on the ground. Happily she rushed, stretching the leash taut, when she saw Donovan bent down to pat her.

"I see who gets consoled first." I laughed, handing him her leash.

"We have to get her settled before I can really console you." He leaned over and gave me a warm, soft, gentle kiss on the forehead.

The inside of his house was an open floor plan. He definitely didn't have the bachelor pad look with empty pizza boxes and beer bottles lying around that Sean had.

The black leather motif worked with the open feel of the modern, combined kitchen-and- family room. Granite countertops and black cabinets added to the elegance.

It felt good to be around a real adult man.

"Sit. I'll take care of her." He gestured for me to sit by the gas fireplace that was roaring, heat coming from it.

He put a doggie bed near the hearth because he knew Willow loved the warmth against her plump pink-and-brown-spotted body. She gladly let him cover her with a small blanket he retrieved from one of the bedrooms.

"There." He walked over to the couch and sat down next to me. His head was a little messed up from sleeping and there were bags under his tired eyes, but he still looked handsome. "How are you?"

He didn't waste anytime to see for himself just how I was.

"Donovan Scott," I pushed him back. His deep brown eyes danced with amusement. "Is this your way of helping a poor defenseless gal?"

"Holly Harper, you are anything but defenseless." He bent back down.

I didn't protest.

For some reason I slept like a baby when I was at Donovan's house. The warm cozy bed was the perfect softness and firmness. Willow didn't have any trouble sleeping either.

The knock at the guest bedroom door was light.

"Are you awake?" Donovan came in carrying a small wooden tray with two cups of steaming coffee on it. Willow chugged along next to him.

"Good morning." I propped myself up on a couple of the pillows and straightened the covers next to me so he could sit down.

"I didn't want to leave without saying good morning." Donovan was dressed in jeans and a polo shirt. His muscles poked out from the sleeve just enough to make the insides of any girl squeal.

He had good hair. Nice and thick. He used just the right amount of gel to give it a good texture. Mature hair. Not like Sean's messy shaggy look.

"I need to get up anyway." I lifted my arms in the air and let out a big yawn.

The clock on the nightstand read six-thirty a.m. I needed to get up and go home to change my clothes before I had to get to work. If my memory served me, I had a few wedding appointments today. Plus I wanted to stop by Second Cup to see Bernadine.

I grabbed my phone that was next to me. I kept it there all night in case Bernadine needed to call me.

He sat the tray on the nightstand and handed me a cup of coffee before he sat down and took his cup.

"Do you think Noah is going to pay you a visit today?" he asked.

Last night after our little make-out session, I told Donovan about Noah and how nosey Officer Kiss had told him about the beading tool. I was curious to know what tool she was talking about.

"I guess." I shrugged and let the warm liquid start to wake me up. "There is no way the tool was mine. I order mine. And the tools I use are the high-end ones that are only sold by wholesalers to legitimate companies like The Beaded Dragonfly."

Everything I got for the bead shop was ordered through online wholesale companies. Sure, anyone could go to their local Michael's or Wal-Mart to pick up some of the cheaper beading products, but my products were top of the line.

"I'm not worried." I shook the notion of being a suspect out of my head. "It should be easy to show him my products verses the cheap ones."

"Do you think Bernadine did it?" Donovan asked as if he had on kid gloves.

"Why would you say that?" I laughed, putting the silly notion to rest. "She had no reason." I stopped. "Though he was taking her back to court for a change in his alimony." I shook my head. "That's silly. Bernadine would never hurt a flea, but I can't rule out he didn't have enemies."

"Like who?" Donovan prodded.

"Well. . ." I thought for a second. "I'm not sure. I don't know him that well. He's only been here for a few months."

"That is what you and Bernadine need to figure out." Donovan stood up. "Please come to class tonight. I'm worried about you."

"I think I will." I smiled and let him give me a good kiss that would fill me up for the day.

Chapter Six

After Donovan left to teach his college classes for the day, Willow and I left, thinking about Donovan's question about whom Henry could have pissed off.

The thought of someone stabbing him sent chills through me. That seemed like a terrible way to die.

I turned around and looked at the grey clapboard, three-room cottage I called home. It was all I needed after my divorce. Three rooms were big enough for all the stuff I had collected over the years. The best part wasn't the wall of windows that overlooked the lake or the fact that Ginger pays someone to squeegee them, but rather the furniture.

It came fully furnished and the only *Unders* in the entire place were beneath the futon and the claw-foot tub.

The cabinets in the kitchen went all the way down to the floor. There wasn't a kitchen table to worry about sweeping under, no book shelves to dust under, no *Unders* whatsoever.

There were built-in bookshelves in the family room. The bedroom was plain and simple with just a box spring and mattress. The closet was all I needed for what little clothes I was fitting into at the time.

After feeding Willow, I went and ran a bath in the tub. It felt like a good soaking morning to help melt the stress away.

I even filled it with bubbles right up to the top. I emerged myself as deep as I could and closed my eyes.

Who could Henry have pissed off? I ran the question around in my head.

He had lived here a little bit before the divorce, but not long enough to open his practice. Henry Frisk was a dentist. He was in his fifties and not all that bad looking from what I remembered.

Just last week he had come into the shop to see Bernadine. They had a few words outside but she didn't say anything about them fighting or having words.

"Kevin Russell." I plunged my body forward. The water teetered over the sides of the tub.

I ran my tongue along the front of my teeth. I faintly remembered Agnes saying something about overhearing Dr. Russell and Henry having words at the Barn Dance committee meeting. And why was Henry at the meeting? Was he on the committee?

The committee was comprised of all the business owners in Swanee. In fact, Bobbi Hart, who was in charge of the Barn Dance had come by the bead shop asking if I wanted to be on the committee and be a sponsor. I sent her away because any extra money I had went toward the shop. She was a little off-put by me not participating and didn't bother trying to hide her dislike for my decision to not be on a committee. Gossip in Swanee spread like wildfire. And I was the about the only store owner not on a Barn Dance committee.

But maybe it was time to reconsider her offer.

After my epiphany of Dr. Russell's hatred toward Henry and that it was a possible motive, I jumped out of the tub and threw on some black yoga pants and a hot pink knit top along with my running shoes. It was a perfect combination for working around the shop, meeting with potential brides, and Donovan's self-defense class.

Willow was snoring away in her bed. There wasn't any sense in disturbing her. She'd be fine at home for the day since she used a litter box to do her business. I left the TV on Animal Planet so she'd have a little company.

I grabbed my bag, cell, keys, and jumped into my car heading it toward downtown Swanee.

Since I had opened The Beaded Dragonfly, many new shops have started to revitalize the downtown area. Swanee was hit by the recession and most small businesses had to shut down.

When I drove down Main Street, I slowed down in front of my best friend's house, Ginger Sloan Rush. She had been an honorary Diva until just recently when she came to her senses and divorced the criminal, making her a full Diva.

Anyway, Ginger had gone on a couple-months-long vacation to the U.S. Virgin Islands to get away and was due home anytime. Unfortunately, it didn't look like anyone was home so I headed on down the road.

The old brick buildings that were three stories high lined the main downtown area of Swanee. Bernadine had gotten a great deal on the last building on the right side of Main Street. It was a perfect setting for a café-style coffee shop with the small round wrought iron tables and chairs to match inside the white picket fencing she had Sean install around the side of the building.

Instead of a sign hanging off the building, Bernadine had an iron arm that extended over the sidewalk with an amazing chandelier hanging from it. It was all sorts of fancy and that was exactly what Bernadine wanted.

The inside of the shop screamed fancy too, but the prices reflected differently. Sean had restored the exposed brick, giving it a warm feeling. Bernadine had the menu posted behind the counter on a wall-length chalkboard. Instead of putting down new flooring, Bernadine cleaned up the old orange tiles and laid large oriental rugs all over them. She had gotten several of them from estate sales and local yard sales. Plus Agnes Pearl had a few in her attic she donated.

The seating inside was like sitting down at home for a cup of coffee. On one side of the shop, she had old, broken-in leather furniture all catawampus giving a comfy place to relax. On the other side there were several large and small farm tables surrounded by several non-matching chairs. She used fresh-cut wildflowers in mason jars and red placemats on each table giving it a homey feel.

The counter was the typical glass counter with all sorts of treats inside. Bernadine was an excellent pastry chef and used her talents before Henry had brought her to Swanee.

My very favorite feature of the new shop was the different styles of teapots that Sean had hung as light fixtures. Instead of the typical can-lights or pendant lighting, Bernadine had a great idea to use them and it

added just the final touch of cozy Second Cup was known for.

"Good morning," Bernadine called from behind the counter.

Her luscious red hair was pulled back into a loose pony. Her jade eyes dipped down into dark bags. She obviously didn't get much sleep, which I had hoped she would have since I gave her a few sleeping pills and left when she was sawing logs.

She waved me over. Her clothes were perfect like always.

I made my way through the crowd. Mornings were always so busy, but today was especially busy.

"Gosh, you are busy today." I rolled up on my toes to get a look at what everyone was gawking over.

"Those new Food Watchers low-fat products are selling like hot cakes," Sadie May said, "I'm so glad you are here." She flung a hand towel over her shoulder. She tucked a piece of brown hair behind her ear, barely long enough to stay in place. "You need to get her out of here. Everyone is asking her about Henry."

Sadie and her husband, Gilley, were new to Swanee. Gilley was hired as a new officer with the Swanee police alongside Beverly and Noah. Gilley didn't look like your typical police officer with his purple Mohawk.

"I thought I would come by to see what I could do." I smiled, looking down at the five-foot-tall Sadie.

When Bernadine opened Second Cup, Sadie was excited because she had just graduated from pastry school, she was new to the area, and needed a job.

She loved coming in at four a.m. to make the goodies, while Bernadine loved to snuggle in her California-king bed.

I got a glimpse of the goodies that were going as fast as Sadie could put them in the glass counter. I still couldn't believe that Bernadine let Ms. Food Watchers put stuff in the café. It wasn't like Ms. Food Watchers was hard up for money.

"Thanks for tucking me in last night." Bernadine brought over two cups of coffee and handed me one. "Unfortunately I woke up about two hours after you left."

Sadie ran her hand down Bernadine's arm. "Why don't you go with Holly for a little bit?"

"I'm fine." Bernadine shook off the notion. "We were divorced. Life has to go on."

Sadie gave a sympathy smile before she ran off to help behind the counter. I followed Bernadine to the back where the kitchen was located. She had a stainless-steel bar-style café table with two tall chairs. She sat in one and I sat in the other.

"Are you sure you are okay?" I sat the steamy cup of coffee in front of me.

The smell of cinnamon, apple, sugar, and chocolate engulfed every single space of air. There was no way I could own or work in an environment like this. I was sure that by osmosis I would be walking out with ten extra pounds on my hips.

"Noah stopped by and asked me some strange questions." Bernadine shook her head.

"Like what?" I didn't bring up the missing crimp tool or the fact that Noah said there was some sort of beading tool at the crime scene. There was no way my tool had just walked its way over to kill Henry.

"He said that Henry was stabbed to death in one of the dental chairs." Her brows lifted. "Of course I never wanted him dead." She bit her lip.

"Bernadine!" Sadie ran to the kitchen, fear set in her big brown eyes. "Noah is here and is closing down the café."

Bernadine jumped up knocking the chair on the ground. I got up and picked it up. Before we could walk back out into the store area, Noah had made it to the kitchen door.

"Ladies," he greeted us and took off his hat. He tucked the stiff thing under his arm. "Bernadine, I need to have a word with you."

"Don't you dare!" I warned her. "You call Bennie."

"It's just a word." Bernadine let out a nervous laugh. Her chubby cheeks fluttered with uneasiness.

"If it's just a word, then why is Beverly herding everyone out and the sign on the door is turned over to the closed side?" I pointed out my observations of what was going on around us.

Bernadine's brows formed a "V" in concern.

"I'm calling Flora." I plucked my phone from the depths of my bag and clicked on my favorites button.

All the Divas were in my favorites. I hit Flora's name.

"Flora, Henry Frisk was found dead in his office and Noah is at Second Cup shutting the place down."

"Stop right there," Flora interrupted. "I'm calling my bastard right now."

I didn't have to ask whom she was referring to nor did I have time. She had hung up before my heart could take its next beat.

Bernadine and I sat at one of the tables waiting for Bennie to show up. Noah and the other officers did all sorts of counting and fingerprinting, leaving a mess along the way.

Bernadine had chipped off half of her red nail polish before Bennie arrived.

"Sorry, Bennie." Beverly put her hand on Bennie's chest when he tried to enter. She looked like a big giant guarding the place. "Closed."

"Not for me." He shoved past Beverly.

"Are you representing her?" Beverly stood in disbelief. "You have got to be kidding me. Bennie, you won't win this one."

"Bennie." Bernadine jumped up and melted into Bennie's neatly pressed sear-sucker white-and-blue striped jacket. When she pulled away, there was a big mascara stain on the front pocket.

"Let's talk." He gestured to the leather chair on the other side. He took out the hanky from the pocket and started to wipe down the pocket, making the mascara streak more. Finally giving up, he put the hanky back in the pocket. "It's a little more private over here."

Big mouth Beverly must've told Noah Bennie was here because within seconds he was headed our way. There was a plastic evidence bag in his hand. As he got closer, I could tell there was some red stuff in there, like blood. I figured he didn't go to the kitchen for red food coloring.

"Bennie." Noah did the guy nod thing. Bennie did his best to do the guy nod back, but everyone in town knew Bennie was gay and didn't try to be anything different.

"Bennie!" A voice shouted from the front door.

It was Bennie's private investigator, Ernie. He looked like he had just crawled out of bed with his untucked button down. Plus, the two top buttons were undone, not to mention it was wrinkled like it had been balled up in a corner of a room for days. There was a small stain on the thigh of his khaki pants.

At the same time, Bennie and Noah motioned for him to come on over. Reluctantly, Beverly let him through. There was a crowd that had gathered outside and spilled into Main Street. News traveled fast in Swanee and this was big news.

"What's going on in there, Holly?" Agnes tapped on the window and then used it as a shield over her brows to see in better. "I can see you in there!"

Agnes lived in the heart of town in an old mansion like Ginger. She didn't miss a beat. Especially since she just had her eyes fixed.

"Noah Druck, you better tell me what's going on in there or I'm going to call your momma!" Agnes was getting more and more irritate and knocked louder and louder until Noah finally gave in and walked out to talk to her.

Apparently she didn't like what he had to say because she was scolding him, wagging her finger in his face as Noah just stared down at the ground.

Noah walked back in and put his hat on his head.

"I don't know what you feed these women, Holly, but they have all gone nuts since you started that little gossip circle, and nothing but venom is coming from it."

My phone chirped. Thank God because it probably saved me from going to jail for beating up an officer. I

retrieved it to see who it was. It was Cheri. She texted me to tell me that Gilley was there to talk to me. She wanted to know where I was.

"You sent Gilley to The Beaded Dragonfly?" I asked Noah and tried not to stare at the bloody knife in the plastic evidence bag.

"I told you I needed to look at your beading supplies." Noah had a smug look on his face. "Anyway, this is one of the weapons that killed Henry."

Bernadine covered her mouth and looked away. Bennie tried to give her comfort by rubbing her back. Her chest heaved up and down with each little sob.

"When we did our research, we learned these knives are only available to people in the food industry." Noah set the knife on the table. Bennie leaned over and took a look. "We are going to every local restaurant or any establishment that has to do with food and going through their inventory. And since you were his ex-wife and own Second Cup, I figured we'd give you the opportunity to come clean."

"I didn't do it!" Bernadine blurted out.

"Shh." Bennie patted her hand.

"It's no secret that you and that divorced group *love* to bash your ex-husbands. He did in fact divorce you right after you moved here. Then left you here while he moved on with a glamorous life in Fort Myers." Noah read from his notebook where he had dug up the history. "He paid you a lump sum of eight thousand dollars a month in alimony and is currently suing you to lower the alimony."

My mouth was suddenly dry when I heard the eight thousand dollar amount. I knew Bernadine had been taken good care of by Henry's alimony, but I had no idea it was that much. I assumed she was joking yesterday when we were in Food Watchers. Apparently not.

Damn. It wasn't looking good for her. It was no secret the number one reason for murder was money.

"Plus we found a beading tool at the scene. You bead. You have knives. You get eight thousand a month. Why would you kill him?" Noah pulled out a piece of paper and slapped it on the table in front of her.

It was pictures of the bloody crime scene. I had to look away.

"You and your cute little Diva friends come up with all sorts of ways to hurt the men who happened to not want you anymore." Noah stood up and leaned over Bernadine. He played the bad cop card. "Isn't that right, Bernadine Frisk?"

"I never planned on him dying." Bernadine buried her head in her hands.

"So you did stab him to death?" Noah pounded his fist on the table.

"Hold on. My client did no such thing and unless you are charging her for murder, I think it's time I take her home." Bennie stood up and ordered Bernadine to get up too. "You let us know when you are done here. My client has to make a living."

Noah was a cool as a cucumber and tapped the paper lying in front of him.

Bennie whispered a couple of things to Ernie and Ernie shot out of the door. Bernadine grabbed her purse and Bennie escorted us out.

“Now,” Bennie turned toward me. “Let’s get to The Beaded Dragonfly.”

Chapter Seven

Bennie and Bernadine followed me to The Beaded Dragonfly and we were there in mere seconds. Just like Cheri had said, Gilley was at the front door waiting patiently. His Mohawk was tucked up under his police cap.

"Hey, Holly." His eyes dipped down. "I hate to ask you to let me in and let me look through your stuff, but you know it's part of the job."

"Sure." I wasn't going to fight with him. Gilley was a sweet guy and he was so nice. "I have nothing to hide."

"I'm not saying you do, but someone either wants us to believe you do or one of your friends is guilty." He turned when Bernadine and Bennie approached us on the doorstep.

I unlocked the door and ran my hand up against the wall to flick on the lights. Cheri must've have been waiting by the window in her apartment because she bolted down the back stairs and met us on the bead store floor.

"Here is the tool that was found at the scene." Gilley took the bag out of his shirt and unrolled it.

I gasped. Noah was right. The Eurotool crimping tool I specifically used in the store, the one that was missing, was in the bag.

"I'm assuming you know this tool?" Gilley asked. "We know that this specific tool has to be ordered by a lapidary with a tax id number."

"Oh my God," Bernadine mumbled. "I did not take that tool from here."

"I know." I tried to quiet her down. "Bennie and Ernie will figure this all out."

"The only thing really saving you at this point, Ms. Frisk, is that we don't have any fingerprints." Gilley stopped talking. "I probably shouldn't have told you that, but I know what Sadie tells me about you and it just doesn't add up. But the evidence does speak for itself."

Bennie pulled Bernadine aside.

"Can I take a look at your inventory and what your sheets say you have?" Gilley asked and put the crimp tool back in his jacket.

"Sure." I walked behind the counter where I kept the inventory sheets and cringed a little. That was one of Marlene's jobs and she liked to talk when she did inventory so I wasn't sure on how accurate it was. I wasn't about to tell Gilley that I was in fact missing a crimp tool just like the bloody one in the bag.

The thought of someone from the group taking my tool didn't sit well with my gut. I was going to have to question every single Diva in the group.

Gilley took the three-ring spiral inventory notebook from me and disappeared into the back with Cheri.

I quickly texted all the Divas to let them know we had an emergency Diva meeting tonight at six p.m. I didn't have any beading classes and closing an hour earlier wasn't going to hurt anyone. Besides, Bernadine was in more need than us and I had to figure out who took those crimpers.

"Holly Harper!" Marlene bolted through the door. Feathers from her hot pink boa flew all over the place. Briefly stopping inside the door, she wrapped it around her neck several times. "What on God's green earth is going on around here? Agnes Pearl came home confused as a two dollar hooker with a fifty dollar bill." Marlene leaned up against the counter trying to catch her breath. She must've ran the whole couple blocks down here.

"What did she say?" I was curious to see what Noah had told her.

"She said that Noah Druck told her Henry Frisk was killed and he was looking into talking to Bernadine." Marlene's eyes creased with worry. "Which doesn't make sense since they were divorced. Why would Bernadine care?"

The unanswered question hung between us until Marlene's mouth formed an O. She looked between me and Bernadine, who was in the corner talking to Bennie.

"That no good son of a bitch." Spit came out of Marlene's mouth. "I forgot he was taking her back to court." She leaned in a little closer and whispered, "But do you think she killed him because of it?"

"No." I blew off the notion. "She wouldn't hurt a flea."

"Holly?" Gilley came out from the storage room. "Hi, Marlene."

"Gilley." Marlene's mouth couldn't seem to stay shut. "What are you doing here?"

He ignored her.

"Mr. White?" Gilley got Bennie's attention. "There seems to be a pair of Holly's crimp tools missing from her stock and we found this one at the scene of Dr. Frisk. Does your client want to make a statement before I write my report?"

"No." Bennie grabbed Bernadine by the elbow.

Bernadine glanced over her shoulder at me before Bennie shoved her out of the front door of the shop. She clamped her jaw tight and stared. Fear, stark and vivid, glittered in her eyes.

Chapter Eight

It wasn't long after Bennie, Bernadine, and Gilley left before Flora and Agnes made their way to the shop.

"I said six p.m. not nine a.m." I turned the closed sign on the door to open.

It was still business as usual.

"Even though Bennie did me dirty, he knows he better help Bernadine." Flora used her fingertips to style her brown wavy hair. Her big cheekbones had the perfect amount of rouge on them. She sat her Fendi bag on the beading table. "When you called this morning, I was getting my hair done and all the girls were talking about the fight between Kevin and Henry. You know how gossipy salons can be. But I told Bennie anyway. Just in case it was important." She blew on her nails. "Charlotte told me that Kevin even threw a punch."

Flora had a standing appointment with Charlotte every week to get her hair and nails done. Flora said that being fifty years old was just a number. She kept herself in shape. Even though she loved to bash Bennie, she said she'd still like to find love one day.

"I immediately dialed Babbs to get a hold of Ernie." She stopped blowing on her fingers briefly. Babbs was Bennie's secretary.

Flora's cell chirped. Gingerly and with her fingertips, she pulled the phone from the side pocket of her purse, careful not to get nail polish on the expensive bag.

"Hello?" She excused herself from the shop and went in the back to talk on her phone.

"What is going on? I leave town for a couple months and come back to this?" Ginger Sloan Rush surged through the door. The jingle bells flung around creating all sorts of noise as the door flew open. "Marlene."

Ginger's eyes zeroed in on Marlene. It wasn't a secret that Ginger had her doubts about Marlene and had practically given her a grand inquisition when Marlene showed up in Swanee. It was unusual for people to just appear and start a life here since most of the town was born and bred here.

There was never a time I was so happy to see her. The trip did her good. Her long dark hair hung over her shoulder in long graceful curls. There was a hint of tan on her cheeks. Her blue eyes popped behind her thick well-manicured brows. She must really be sun kissed, because her teeth were so bright against her lips.

"You look great!" I came from behind the counter and gave her a big hug. "I went by your house this morning. It didn't look like you were home."

"I wasn't. I got in town a few minutes ago and you know gossip spreads like the flu around Swanee." She tilted her head to the side and nodded toward Marlene who was stocking the new merchandise she didn't do from yesterday. "Marlene didn't cap Henry, did she?"

"Wishful thinking on your part?" I laughed and winked. "But all joking aside, I think Bernadine is in trouble."

Flora, who was still outside on the phone, tapped on the window. “Be back later,” she mouthed and waved bye.

“Tell me what you know.” She planted her butt in one of the bead chairs.

I told her all about the missing crimpers and how it was there before the Wine and Bead class started because I was the one who counted them out for the twelve of us there. And I told her about Kevin and Henry’s fight at the Barn Dance committee meeting.

“Really?” Ginger tapped her temple with her finger. “I belong on that committee.”

Which wasn’t a big revelation to me since her family did own half of Swanee.

“Maybe me and you should go by the financial meeting tonight because Kevin Russell is the chairman of that particular committee on the Barn Dance Board.”

“Great! I’ve been beating myself up all night for not accepting the invitation to join when they were asking all the businesses,” I said. “Even if we could just see his demeanor.”

"Surely Noah Druck is checking him out," Marlene said as she broke down the empty boxes. "I put the invoices on the counter over there."

"Just think about it." Ginger stood up. Her long lean legs looked thinner in the dark skinny jeans. She wore a white blouse tucked in with the collar up and strands of pearls dripping down the front at all different lengths. "Henry Frisk comes to town. He has those massaging chairs in the cleaning rooms, a Keurig coffee maker in the lobby for clients to enjoy, and he gives away that amazing bag of swag."

"How do you know of this?" I asked. Marlene stopped dead in her tracks. The only ex we Divas associated with was Bennie. He had resources we needed.

Her face reddened deeper than her tan. She swallowed hard.

"Well," she hesitated.

"Ginger," I coaxed her. "You didn't," I gasped and put my hand over my mouth.

"It was his first week here before I left and I'm the chair of Swanee's Welcoming Committee." She put her hand up to her chest.

"Since when did Swanee get a welcoming committee?" I looked at her suspiciously. "No one ever came to welcome me when I opened The Beaded Dragonfly."

"Since the revitalization of downtown, the City Council felt that we needed to make sure the new businesses feel welcome." She ran her tongue across her extra shiny white teeth. "Anyway, he was way more charming than Bernadine gave him credit for and he is devilishly handsome and young up close."

My mouth dropped, my nose snarled.

Marlene eased herself in the chair on the opposite side of the table.

"Too bad he's dead." Marlene stuck her elbows on the table and rested her chin in her hands.

Marlene loved them rich and hot. Two things that were lacking in the men who lived in Swanee.

"Anyway," Ginger ignored Marlene, "he asked me to come in to see the office. He showed me how the massage chair worked. When I sat down, I melted. He threw on a mask, whipped that light over my eyes and he illuminated like an angel staring down at me with those big puppy dog eyes."

We all gave a little sigh.

"When he said he'd give me a complimentary cleaning that would keep me coming back, he was right." She opened her lips real wide and showed her teeth. "He did a beautiful job. I couldn't stop staring at his flawless skin and lovely eyes."

"But he's Bernadine's ex." Everything Ginger said was mesmerizing, but the fact still remained that he was an ex-ass.

"I know. That is why I never said anything." Her jaw tensed. "Then he ordered surveillance equipment. Which reminds me, I need to check with Joni to see if it was installed."

"Surveillance equipment?" A spark ignited. "If he had some sort of camera and he was killed in the office, it would show it!"

"Don't be going and getting excited." Ginger looked at her watch. "We are so far behind on installation and I took that trip which didn't help move things quicker. The system for Henry's office wasn't even going to be installed until a couple weeks from right now. Though I did put him on the cancellation list."

"You need to check that out and we need to figure out if some of Kevin's clients were being wooed away from his office like Henry obviously wooed you." My wheels were turning.

"Too bad he's dead." Ginger's eyes lowered. "He really did a good job on my teeth. And he said that the next time I come back, they don't take co-pays. He will bill your insurance for the full amount."

"No co-pay?" That almost sounded too good to be true. I stood up when the ten o'clock bridal appointment came in. "I have a business to run and you have to go talk to Joni. Be back here by six p.m. to meet up with the Divas."

Marlene got up and greeted the bride and the other girl with her. There was a full list of questions I had come up with so I could create the perfect jewelry for the wedding.

"We have to be at the financial meeting by seven." Ginger reminded me.

"Seven?" Inwardly I groaned. That was the time for self-defense class. There was no way I could go there and the meeting. The meeting was definitely more important. "We can go together."

"See you at six. Or I'll call you before if I find anything else out about you-know-what." She gave the spirit wave over her shoulder before she walked out.

The you-know-what was video of a murderer stabbing Henry to death. Even if there was something like that there, Noah would have already seen it. But you never know.

I found that a woman on a mission to find out something was far better than an FBI agent. I didn't know who had stolen my crimpers, but I did know one thing, Bernadine Frisk was too tidy and neat to get blood on her hands.

Chapter Nine

"Welcome to The Beaded Dragonfly." I held my hand out to shake the girls' hands. I wasn't sure which one was the bride. "I see you have met my assistant Marlene."

Marlene nodded.

"This is Autumn," Marlene gestured toward the petite blonde. I should've known she was the bride because they always look so gaunt and thin from starving themselves for their big day.

"This is Jenna, my maid of honor," Autumn introduced the meat-on-the-bones, average-size young woman next to her.

They couldn't be any more than twenty-five. Sometimes the lovestruck look on the happy brides-to-be faces made me sick. If they only knew what was in store for them. A life of cheating, long nights alone, and chocolate. Lots and lots of chocolate.

I kept my mouth shut and planted a big ole happy smile on my face.

"There isn't anything better than a wonderful wedding and happy marriage." I glanced over at Marlene. "Isn't that right?"

Huh. Marlene wasn't good at faking it.

"Right, *Marlene*?"

"Whatever you say, Holly." Marlene disappeared into the back and brought out the chocolate-covered strawberries and two flutes of champagne to give to the girls.

It was something I had seen on the Wedding Channel. I knew that after Margaret McGee's wedding every girl in Swanee and surrounding counties would be coming here to see exactly what I had to offer. A little bit of expense to show them The Beaded Dragonfly was a classy place was just the icing on the cake for a big sale.

"I'll let you two help yourself to the treats while you fill out your forms." I guided them to the bridal table that was specifically set up for such appointments.

The sunlight beamed through the large floor-to-ceiling windows. The beads glistened throughout the shop. I had several pieces displayed on the table and the sun's rays hit the jewelry perfectly, making them shine to the brilliance that would almost hurt your eyes if you stared at the beauty too long. That was another little trick I learned on the Wedding Channel.

The girls smiled and took their place at the bride's table and I pulled Marlene to the side.

"Do you think you could finish the first meeting with Autumn?" The phone rang. I put my hand on it and finished my sentence. "I'm going to see Bobbi Hart and see if I can get on that Barn Dance Committee."

I plucked the phone receiver off the wall.

"The Beaded Dragonfly," I answered in a chirpy voice.

"Holly, it's Carol from Dr. Russell's office. I wanted to follow up on our conversation from last night and I have a couple openings for your cleaning," she said. I could hear a page crinkling in the background like she was flipping a schedule book. "We have to get you in here to keep those beautiful teeth white and I also wanted to say that I can tell you have lost some weight."

"Oh, Carol. That is so kind." Compliments always made me melt. . .even if it did come from the dental receptionist. I looked down into the glass counter, opened my lips with my teeth clinched. They could stand a scrub. "What are your openings?"

"We have a cancellation today."

Damn.

"Can you be here in about ten minutes?" she asked.

"Umm. . ." My eyes bugged out of my head and I glanced over at Marlene. "Can you hold on?"

"Sure," Carol agreed.

I covered the mouth of the phone with my hand.

"Marlene, this is Carol from Dr. Russell's office and they have a dental cleaning opening in ten minutes. Do you think you could stay here longer than the time it would take me to talk to Bobbi?"

Marlene danced on her toes. She clasped her hands together in delight. "You work fast." She winked. "Skipping the committee gossip and going straight to the source."

"What?" My face contorted in confusion.

"Dr. Russell and Henry's fight?" Marlene reminded me about the information I could probably get out of Dr. Russell if I was sitting in his chair.

"Carol, I'll see you in ten," I confirmed and hung up the phone. "Marlene, I was so nervous about the cleaning that I completely forgot about the fight." I placed my hands on her shoulders. "You are a genius!"

I grabbed my bag and left Marlene in charge of the shop. She'd be fine and she could certainly handle the bride's first appointment since it was only a fact gathering session on what Autumn had in mind and the colors.

It didn't take me long to drive over to Dr. Russell's. The lot was empty. The brown, square, brick, stand-alone boring building had minimal landscape with the small bushes going around the entire office. There were two long and wide windows on each side of the door with the old metal horizontal blinds that had yellowed over the years from the sun.

I pushed the door open and immediately the sterile stale smell of rubber and band-aids made my stomach curl. The old wood paneling hung from the waiting room walls. Carol's sliding glass window was cracked. There was a clipboard teetering off the edge where clients checked in.

Ahem. I cleared my throat when I didn't see Carol behind the glass. I took the pen that was tied to the clip on the clipboard with a string of yarn and wrote my name down on the page that had the date printed very large on the top.

I flipped through the week's worth of pages. I inwardly groaned when I saw Charlie's name. She'd been here a couple of days ago. But the most disturbing thing was *not* seeing a lot of names on each page. I was used to signing the paper and seeing members of the community on there.

I put the board back on the edge and took a seat in one of the old plastic vinyl chairs that had cracks in all of them. I picked the one with the fewest cracks and didn't expose the padding underneath.

"Hi, Holly." Carol flung the window open and grabbed the clipboard. "Anything change on your insurance?" she asked and crossed off my name.

"All the same." I smiled and picked up an Oprah magazine from two years ago. I put it back when I realized I looked at it the last time I was here.

Ginger's description of Henry Frisk's dental office played in my head. I'd kill to have a Keurig cup of coffee right now. There definitely wasn't a complimentary Keurig machine in Kevin's office, and I would bet the same grey plastic pod dental chairs were in the back too.

"How has business been?" I asked Carol, trying to get some information out of her.

"Meh," she curled her nose. "It had slowed down a lot since Henry Frisk opened a couple months ago. But since

the," she ran her finger along her neck, "clients have called to schedule."

"Yeah, that was terrible." I let out a long sigh and eyed her reaction.

"It was. I have been looking over my back and catching myself checking the locks on my windows and doors at home several times before I go to bed." She shook her head. Her lips dipped. "I just don't know why someone would go around killing someone. Dr. Frisk always seemed nice when he stopped by."

"He would come by here?" I asked.

That seemed odd. Why would Henry want to come see his competition? There were plenty of teeth to clean and dentures to fix from all the good citizens of Swanee to go around.

"Between me and you." Carol stood up. She glanced behind her as if she was checking to see if the coast was clear. "I don't think he and Dr. Russell liked each other. Dr. Frisk came in before he opened his shop and told Dr. Russell out of courtesy that he was going to open an office. I didn't see a problem with it, but Dr. Russell was spitting mad all day after that."

"What did he say about it?" I stood up and walked over.

"He didn't say anything." Her eyes grew as big as the sun. "He slammed his door, cussed, threw things and made clients bleed."

"Bleed?" My heart pumped. I held my hand to my chest hoping that blood wasn't going to come out of my gums after this cleaning.

"Clients called to tell me he had done a deep cleaning and made them bleed more than normal." She rolled her eyes. "I couldn't tell them he was mad and was probably taking it out on them."

I clenched my teeth together. They were already hurting.

"Oh don't worry." Carol smiled. "He's been in a great mood the last couple of days. You will be fine."

"Do you mean he's been in a good mood since?" I ran my finger along my neck.

Slowly she nodded.

"Good morning, Holly." Dr. Russell appeared at the waiting room door. "Are you ready?" he asked. His rubbery lips sat below his beaklike nose on his thin long face. His scraggly brows dipped. "Holly?"

"Um. . ." I hesitated. "Ready as I'll ever be." I stood up and walked through the door.

The stinky smell of the office almost made me faint. The seventies orange wall-to-wall carpet was in desperate need of an overhaul. The wallpaper had the fuzzy textured look, but most of the fuzzy had long been rubbed off.

"How is your shop?" he asked and pointed for me to sit.

"Great. I have been doing a lot of brides since Margaret's wedding." That was probably the last time I had seen Dr. Russell. He and his wife had sat in the corner the entire night.

I was right. The old dental chair was there. I sat down. He took the old blue plastic, paper bib combination and used the silver clips to hold it in place around my neck.

He snapped on latex gloves and ran his finger from each hand down the other for a snug fit.

I took several deep breaths to try to help slow down my racing heart. I kept my eyes ahead. The air from the pleather cushion of the rolling dental chair swooshed as he sat down on it. The wheels squeaked across the floor as he got closer.

"That's great. My wife had mentioned she wanted to try that Wine and Bead class or something like that." He flipped the big spotlight above my head on and pulled it over top of me. He lowered my chair.

"She should. Tell her to come on by for a free class." Nervously I opened my mouth as his fingers came closer.

Patsy Russell had to be a good fifteen years younger than Dr. Russell. She was a born and bred southern woman through and through. She never left her house without her pearls: the strand draped down her neck, wrapped around her wrist and stuck in her ears. She was always dressed like she was going to the Kentucky Derby.

A one-piece, one-color dress, heels to match and a hat to complete the outfits.

Once I had overheard her say that she was a doctor's wife and she would rather be caught dead than in sweatpants. I just so happened to be wearing sweatpants that day.

"How has your business been?" I asked, not thinking that a killer's hands could be in my mouth.

"It's picking up," he said. His stale coffee breath nearly knocked me out. "Since Dr. Frisk was found violently killed." He shook his head. His grey eyes were busy looking around my mouth as he took his fingers and spread my lips away from my gums in all sorts of directions.

"I 'eard 'bout 'hat." My speech slurred as I tried to talk back to him.

"It's a shame too." His fingers left my mouth and he picked a tool from the small platter just to his left. "Just a few days ago we were at the Barn Dance Committee meeting and he had some great ideas, but they couldn't be implemented this year since the Barn Dance is coming up.

He didn't understand that and said he would put it together."

"Like what?" I asked before he put that scraping tool in my mouth.

"He wanted to bring a famous country band to play, but the cost was just too much for the financial committee to come up with." The tool scraped up and down my teeth. He used the suction tool to suck up my saliva. "When I told him it wasn't in the budget, he went crazy. He said that he was coming into some extra money and would be more than happy to pay for it. When I asked him when he was going to get the money, he said something about after he won some court case." Dr. Russell shook his head. "If some client was suing him, it could take years to get that money. It wasn't a gamble I was going to take with the Barn Dance budget."

Was a client suing him? Was that why he was taking Bernadine back to court? Was that why he moved back to Swanee?

"Oh, I'm sorry Dr. Russell." A lively female voice came from the right side of me near the door. I couldn't see her since I was practically on my back, scraping tool in my mouth and eyes blinded by the old spotlight. "I didn't see Carol out there and I didn't know you had a client."

I recognized the voice, but couldn't place it.

"Don't worry." Dr. Russell picked up the little metal mirror tool and rotated it all over my mouth and ran it along my gum lines, causing the sides of lips to open wider. Spit dribbled out of the corners of my mouth. "I'll be with you in a few minutes if you want to hang out in my office."

"Sounds great." The woman's voice was happy. "You are going to love the new designs I have put together."

"Looking forward to it." His grey eyes looked down at me. With one hand still in my mouth, he used his other hand to wipe my mouth with the bib.

"Gettin' a 'ew offish." I tried to talk with his fingers in my mouth.

Dr. Russell flipped the spotlight off and swung it over to the opposite side of my head to get it out of the way. He sat my chair up and rolled backward on the stool to the small counter where the tiny sink was. He stood up and took out a small white cup and put fluoride in it setting it next to the sink. I took the bib and wiped my mouth off. My lips felt like they had been stretched over the entire state.

"Go ahead and rinse." Dr. Russell was writing all over my chart. "See you in six months."

"Maybe before that." I slid out of the chair and walked over to the sink. I held the tiny cup in my fingers. "I'm going to see Bobbi Hart to see if I can get on one of the Barn Dance Committees." I took the fluoride like a shot glass and swished it around before I spit it out.

"I think we have room on the decorating committee." He plucked the gloves off his hands and tossed them in the garbage. He held his hand out. "Good seeing you, Holly."

I extended my hand. His cold clammy hand made me gag to think they were just in my mouth and maybe what had been gripped around the knife that killed Henry Frisk.

Chapter Ten

Dr. Russell slipped out of the cleaning room and into his office before I could clean myself up and see who the woman was that was there to see him before she shut the door. I grabbed my bag and headed back down to the waiting room to check out with Carol.

"How was it?" Carol wiped the corners of her mouth with the napkin. Her Big Mac in front of her looked really good. Unfortunately there was no way I could partake. That would add the pound I had lost at Food Watchers.

"It was fine." I reached in my bag and took out my wallet. "Here is my check card for the co-pay."

"Oh, new policy." She took a gulp of the sweet tea. "We are going to bill it all to your insurance so no co-pay."

Ginger said the same thing about Henry. Did Dr. Russell get the same idea from Henry? I could only wonder.

"Say," I gripped my check card and leaned over, "is the place getting a makeover?"

"Yes," Carol gasped. "Can you believe it? I've been telling Dr. Russell for years, but he never listened to me. Then all of the sudden he wants all this fancy stuff. He even hired an interior decorator."

"Yeah, I heard the salesperson come in."

"She did?" Carol's mouth dropped. "She's early. Oh God, was Kevin mad?"

"No, *Kevin* wasn't mad." I drew back and stared at her. For as long as I had been coming here, I had never heard Carol refer to Dr. Russell as Kevin. "I've been meaning to get some quotes on The Beaded Dragonfly. Do you happen to have the interior decorator's name and number?"

"I do." Carol used her finger to flip through the desk calendar. "I told Dr. Russell that we needed to get a computer so I didn't have to keep all of these files."

She licked her finger and grabbed a piece of paper. She wrote down the name and number I had asked for and handed it to me.

"You don't have a computer?" I thought it was strange the doctor wouldn't invest in the latest technology, but then we were talking about Dr. Russell who didn't have anything new.

"No," she sighed. "I still hand write every single appointment and type all of his notes." She rolled her eyes before she took another bite of her sandwich.

"Well." I tapped the piece of paper on my hand before I stuck it in my bag. "I guess I'll see you at the dance."

"I don't think I'm going this year," Carol said. "I've got too much work to do." She pointed over to the stack of papers on the credenza behind her desk.

"Okay. I will see you in six months." I waved over my shoulder.

I didn't recognize the name of the interior decorator Carol had written down. But I knew Bernadine would. Before I went to see Bobbi, I decided to call Bernadine.

"How are you?" I asked her when she answered the phone.

"They let me reopen the shop and Sadie insisted I go home." Her voice was low and sad. "I have something to tell you."

"I'm listening." I started the Beetle and looked around the parking lot. The cute yellow Fiat I had seen in the Food Watchers parking lot was here.

"The knife they found that killed Henry." Bernadine started to cry.

"Yes." Thinking about the bloody bag that Noah Druck had laid on the table, sent goose bumps up and down my body.

"Holly," Bernadine sucked in a deep breath. "The knife came from my home."

"What are you saying, Bernadine?" I questioned my friend. "Did you. . ."

"Of course I didn't kill him, but someone did and that someone broke into my house and took my knife to kill him." Bernadine broke out in sobs. "Someone is after me. Someone is trying to frame me."

"Don't worry." I gulped. "Does Noah know that it came from your house?"

"No." She was quick to respond. "But I don't want to say anything over the phone. I called Rush Security and Joni put me on the list to get surveillance cameras installed in the cabin. Only I'm on the waiting list. I'll be behind bars before they get to me and not need them."

"You aren't going to jail. Noah will figure this out." I slid down in my seat when I noticed Charlie from Food Watchers walk out the door of Dr. Russell's office. She had on a short black dress that hugged her body in all the right places. "If Noah can't figure it out, the Divas will."

Charlie jumped in the yellow Fiat and zoomed off, not putting on her seatbelt.

"Hey, I've got to go, but I'll be by and we can take a quick walk around the lake before our emergency Diva meeting at six." I pulled out a little bit after Charlie left and kept some distance between our cars.

"Sounds good." There was a silent pause. "Do you think I need to tell Bennie about this?"

"I would. He doesn't need to say anything to help the cops and maybe he can give the information to Ernie and Ernie can do whatever it is that Ernie does." I continued to keep my distance.

I thought Charlie just worked at Food Watchers, but I guess she also worked as an interior decorator too. At least that was what Dr. Russell thought.

"Say, do you remember the interior decorator Henry used in the new office?" I asked.

"Why? Is it a clue to who did this?" She returned my question.

"No. Charlie from Food Watchers was paying Dr. Russell a visit and Carol said she was the interior decorator redoing his office," I said. "And for some reason I'm following her because I still can't believe how awful she was to me in the bathroom last night."

It dawned on me that Carol didn't say a word about me threatening Charlie in the bathroom. Granted Charlie didn't hear me, but it made me feel better.

"Let me look in my purse for that bill. I almost threw it away."

I could hear the contents of her purse being dumped out onto her glass-top kitchen table. I was used to her doing that. After all, her purses were as big as her.

"Here it is." I could image her using her hands with her fancy rings all along her fingers trying to unwrinkle the thing. "Buskin Designs. All the way in Lexington."

"Lexington?" I looked up and then veered to the left when I realized Charlie had just driven down the highway that leads to Lexington. "Hold on."

I put the phone down, drove with the other and took out the piece of paper Carol had given me. I turned down the next right and pulled over. I wasn't good at multi-tasking. When I put the car in park, my phone tumbled off my leg in between the console and seat. . .into *The Under.*

"Shit, shit, shit!" I yelled and fisted the paper.

I pulled the little lever to fling my seat back, but the phone wasn't visible. There was only one thing to do. Get out and bend over. There was no way I was going to just stick my hand *under* there and pat around. Not that there was a snake under there, but stranger things had happened.

The phone screen was lit up and I could hear Bernadine chirping from it. I kept my eye on the phone and went straight in.

Beep, beep.

"Nice ass!"

"Ouch!" I grabbed something and jumped up. The old junker car kept moving. I waved hi to them the universal way. . .with my middle finger. I looked down at my hand and my phone was not what I had grabbed. It was the dental floss Dr. Russell always hands out at the end of the appointment, only he didn't give me my little bag of goodies today. Nothing elaborate like Ginger had gotten from Henry, but still it was a new toothbrush that I was looking forward to.

The little metal thing where you cut the floss caught the pad of my finger.

"Ugh," I sighed and put the floss in my pocket. God knew how long that had been under there. Probably since the last time I had gone to see Dr. Russell.

"Holly!" Bernadine screamed from under the seat.

I went back in the *Under*, and this time grabbed the phone.

"Sorry, I dropped the damn phone under the seat." I got back in the car and put my seatbelt on.

"Oh, the under." Bernadine knew my deep-set fear. "On the upswing, you got it."

"I did." I turned the Beetle around and headed back to Swanee. "I was going to go pay Bobbi a visit and get on the Barn Dance Committee."

"Why are you doing that?" Bernadine asked.

"I'm not sure and I don't have any evidence, but I think Kevin Russell killed Henry." There, it was out. I was going to wait to tell her at the Diva meeting but I just blurted it out.

"Why?" Bernadine cried out.

I reminded her about their fight and I told her how Carol said he hadn't been busy since Henry was in town. Plus Carol had said business had picked up. And now Dr. Russell was remodeling.

"Just think about it," I told Bernadine. "Henry moves to town and takes clients from Dr. Russell. Dr. Russell is used to living the good life in that big house. Oh!" I had almost forgotten the most important piece of information Dr. Russell disclosed. "Was Henry suing someone other than you for a large amount of money?"

"Not that I know of. But he would gain about eight thousand dollars a month if he didn't have to pay me alimony." Bernadine paused. "I guess I won't be getting that alimony anymore."

"He was seriously paying you eight thousand a month in alimony?" *Man, did I marry the wrong guy,* I thought. Sean couldn't even keep up with the three hundred he had to give me.

"Please don't say anything to any of the Divas. It wasn't like I wanted the money, but the law stated that he had to give me alimony for half the years we were married. And he did invent or create some sort of new cosmetic dental procedure where he got paid a lot of money. He still holds the patent for it. Plus he had a lot of clients that were famous and would travel from all over the world to see him." She sniffed. "That was why he couldn't stay in Swanee. He thought life in a small town would be the relaxation we would need to work on our marriage, but it was unbearable for him with the slow pace plus the non-stroking of his ego. Which we all know much he loved his ego stroked."

Bernadine had alluded to Henry stepping out on her during their marriage, but she never fully disclosed what had happened. She joined the Divas when we were in the "help me get over the depression" stage in the bottom of the church. When our bonds started to form, that was when we laughed and had a great time bashing them.

"Why would he move back?" I questioned.

"He said he was going to retire from the stars." Bernadine gasped, "Oh my God. Holly, he said that Swanee needed a dentist with new technology and he was going to run Dr. Russell out of business. How could I forget that?"

"See. If Henry even implied that to Dr. Russell, it gives Dr. Russell plenty of motive."

"Why would he try to pin it on me?" Bernadine asked. "Surely the fact that Henry was suing me to stop alimony isn't enough motive to kill him."

"It would be if it would be changing your life drastically. That is how Noah would see it and the district attorney would spin it." I had another thought. "Agnes Pearl's nephew is Bradford Pearl. I wonder if she can get some information from him?"

"Great idea." Bernadine had a little bit of hope in her voice.

"Be at The Beaded Dragonfly by six. I'm at the city building and I want to pop in to see Bobbi."

Bernadine and I got off the phone. Many questions swirled in my head. I knew why Dr. Russell would have a motive, but was the alimony a good motive for him to play and use to pin the murder on Bernadine when Bernadine was making her own money with Second Cup? Something wasn't adding up. They only way to keep a close eye on Dr. Russell besides getting a tooth filling was to stay on every single committee he was on for the Barn Dance. Since the Barn Dance was a week away, that meant I was going to be seeing him a lot, if and only if Bobbi Hart let me join after I had totally dismissed her.

Chapter Eleven

By my curvy figure, anyone would guess how much I loved pie. All sorts of pie. But not the pie I was about to eat with Bobbi Hart. Humble Pie.

Bobbi had always been a little sweet on Sean when we were married. I wasn't sure about now since I wasn't around him much. But when we were married, I couldn't say I was the nicest to her. After all, he was my man and she wanted to sink her claws into him. Granted she didn't look like Charlie, but she didn't look like me either. Less curves, no elastic.

Once I remember Sean saying that I'd be perfect if I had a figure like Bobbi's. I've hated her every since. She knew it. I'd put money on it that when she was voted on the City Council—I didn't vote for her, I wrote in a candidate, Agnes Pearl— she knew she wanted to be in charge of the Barn Dance committee. It was right up her alley. She owned the only party planning business in Swanee, The Pink Pecan.

I had to work with her on Margaret McGee's wedding and that was when she asked me if I wanted to be involved with this year's Barn Dance. Of course I said no. There wasn't any chance in hell I was going to go to those meetings and watch her fawn all over Sean.

Since Sean's Little Shack was the only handyman's business in town, he was the one who helped erect the structures and stages for all the events of the weekend. That gave Bobbi Hart all the access she wanted to him and I wasn't going to watch. We were divorced, but it still didn't mean I wanted to watch every other woman in Swanee fall all over him.

I grabbed the multi-colored glass bead stretch bracelet out of the glove box. I kept several in there for promotional tools in case I wanted to hand a few out so people could understand that The Beaded Dragonfly wasn't just a lapidary, but I also sold already made jewelry.

Stretchy was the perfect promotional item since it wasn't made to a specific wrist size and anyone could just slip it right on and fall in love.

I was sure Bobbi Hart was no different. Though she had never bought anything from me, I did see her eyeing the premade items when she came in to ask me if I wanted to fill out the application for the Barn Dance Committee. I wasn't beyond buttering someone up, but going in and eating my words was an all-different event. Hopefully the bracelet would make it taste much sweeter for me.

Bobbi's office was right inside the door of the City Building. Other than being on city council, she also takes care of the bills for the local water company and electric company. There was never a need for Swanee to have all sorts of buildings for different utilities.

There was nothing like living in a small town. Where else in the world could you pay all of your utility bills in one building and catch up on the local gossip all within minutes? Swanee.

"Hi, Bobbi." I walked into the old office.

The old white tile was probably as old as the building and the fluorescent light did nothing for Bobbi's tan.

"If you need to pay a bill, just slip it in the box." She barely looked up from the old wooden desk in the corner of the room as she pointed to the shoe box that had *payments* printed with a sharpie sitting on the counter.

"Actually, I'm here to see you." I twirled the bracelet around my finger hoping the acid reflux would stay down. "I wanted to know if I could join one of the Barn Dance Committees." I put the bracelet on the counter. "And give you this."

The wooden chair squeaked across the floor as Bobbi stood up. She had on a two-piece pantsuit with sterling silver chains dangling down the front. Her long black hair was neatly pulled back into a bun on the top of her head like one of those fashion runway models you see in one of those reality shows. Her defined cheekbones had enough pink on them to give her tanned skin a little more color than brown.

She started toward me. Her coal black eyes narrowed.

"Is this a bribe, Holly Harper?" Her red lips stayed in a line across her face. "Or is this your way of keeping an eye on me and Sean?"

"You and Sean?" I laughed. "We are old news. I'm dating Donovan Scott."

"Who's that?" Bobbi stood a little taller with curiosity written all over her face.

"A college professor and my self-defense instructor." It sure did feel good touting Donovan's credentials of not only being a hunk, but also a smart and strong hunk.

"Good for you." Bobbi pulled the bracelet toward her. "This is pretty."

"Thank you. I thought it would go great with your olive skin." I lied right through my freshly polished teeth. "Try it on." I encouraged her.

The bracelet fit perfectly around Bobbi's wrist. She held it up to the fluorescent lights, which didn't do much for it, but it did make Bobbi smile.

"What about you? Are you dating anyone?" I asked, just trying to bring up idle chitchat before I asked her again about the committee.

"Nah. I had another date with that new dentist in town but he cancelled." She used her pointer finger to roll the bracelet around.

"Another date?" I questioned her.

She had to be talking about Henry Frisk. He was the only new dentist in town. Did Bernadine know that Henry was on the prowl for a new woman?

"He was older. Cute. Successful." Disappointment settled on her face. "We had a date scheduled and I went to The Livin' End with some of the girls here and Bradford." She stopped. If she blinked, I swear a tear would have fallen down her cheek. "And the guy was there in the dark corner smooching all over someone else. Younger. Prettier. All the parts in the right places if you know what I mean." Bobbi tapped the sides of her thighs.

"I'm so sorry."

"Oh, I got him back." Her eyes rose up to meet mine. They narrowed, her grin got bigger. "I walked right up to him and planted a big kiss on his lips, telling him I was looking forward to our next date."

"Oh my God!" I started laughing.

"That pretty young blonde jumped up and smacked him right across the face." She wagged her finger at me. "You know that sonofabitch must've pissed off the wrong person because someone found him dead." She ran her finger along her neck like it was a knife. "Is it true he was Bernadine Frisk's ex?"

"So it was Henry that you had dated?"

"Yep." She rubbed her hands along the bracelet. "He sure was a good talker. I heard Bernadine is the prime suspect."

"Who said that?" My head popped back. A "V" formed between my brows as if I had no idea what she was talking about.

"Noah Druck came in here asking all sorts of questions about my date. He said he got my name from a piece of paper off Henry's desk. And he wanted to know about the girl Henry was with." The phone rang. Bobbi talked faster. "Evidently, he's looking for her since she was the last person he was seen with." Bobbi held her finger in the air for me to wait. "Barn Dance Committee can you hold?" She asked the person on the other end. She covered the receiver with the palm of her hand. "Come to the gazebo in the park for the committee meeting tomorrow night at six. The Mayor is having the courthouse made over so we are meeting on the lawn before the decorating committee puts the final touches at the barn."

"I'll be there." I clapped my hands and tucked the little bit of information she gave me in the back of my head.

I quickly called Marlene and asked her if she was okay and the shop hadn't burned down. She said everything was good and there was a new bride consultation for the next morning. I told her I needed to go home and let Willow out. I didn't tell her that I was going to pop in Bernadine's first and give her all the information Bobbi

Hart had given me. Especially the part about her and Henry going on dates.

I gripped the steering wheel while driving the curvy back roads to our neck of the woods. We lived in what Swanee residents would call the country part of town. The time passed quickly as I went over all the information I had collected today.

Not only was my appointment with Dr. Russell disturbing, but the fact that Henry was dating was also nagging at me. Who was this other girl? Plus I wanted to be sure that Agnes asked Bradford about it since he was with Bobbi that night at The Livin' End.

"Hey," I called Bernadine on my way over. "I have an hour or so to kill before I need to get back to the shop for a bridal appointment. I'm going to let Willow out. Do you want to take a quick walk?"

"That would be great," Bernadine said. "I'll row right over."

Bernadine was notorious for using her little metal boat to row across the lake to come see me. She insisted that we always start our walks at my house so she could get more exercise rowing back and forth.

Within minutes, I pulled into my gravel drive and could see that her boat had already been dragged up on the lake beach right behind my house. I didn't bother getting my key out because I knew Bernadine had already used my hidden spare key to let herself in. She and Willow were sitting on the couch eating carrots from her baggie.

"You aren't going to believe what I found out." I could hardly contain the news. I grabbed my tennis shoes and tied them up before I grabbed Willow's diamond-studded pink leash off the hook by the door in the kitchen.

"I hope it's something to help clear me of murder." Bernadine crunched down on a carrot and tossed Willow the other end. "Noah Druck came to the house after we had gotten off the phone. He wanted to come in but I said he couldn't without a warrant." She tapped her temple. "I learned something on the CSI show."

"Come on, girl." I coaxed my lazy little piggy up to her hooves. I tugged on the leash to get her away from Bernadine's snack pack.

Bernadine got up and followed my lead. We headed out the door and down toward the beach area.

"Did you know that Henry was dating?" I asked Bernadine.

"Dating?" Bernadine laughed. She huffed as her arms pumped back and forth. "Pump and squeeze, Holly."

Bernadine had all sort of little tricks she blurted out when we walked. She said pumping our arms back and forth helped with blood flow to the heart and squeezing our butt-cheeks helped get rid of cellulite. I wasn't sure if any of it worked, but doing something was better than nothing.

"Yes. He had been on a few dates with Bobbi Hart." I pumped hard and furious. I thought I left Bernadine in the dust, but I turned around and she had stopped.

"Bobbi Hart?" Bernadine's eyes were nearly popped out of her head. Her mouth was gaped open.

I walked back to where she had stopped. "I guess you didn't."

"Is that what she told you?" Her eyes squinted, her lips pinched. "Bobbi Hart is not Henry's type."

"What is his type?" I asked.

"Fuller figure." She ran her hands down her thick waist. "Red hair." She tossed her long curls behind her shoulders and started to walk again. "Squeeze, pump, squeeze, pump," she repeated.

"I know this might be a hard pill to swallow, but he and Bobbi went on a few dates. As a matter of fact," I huffed and puffed. Bernadine must've gotten a sudden spurt of energy because I was having a hard time keeping up. "She saw Henry at The Livin' End with some blonde bombshell the night he was killed."

"That is not possible." Bernadine refused to believe me.

"People saw them. Including Bradford Pearl." I knew if I threw out his name, she'd believe me. After all, he'd be the one to bring charges against the suspect.

"That nogoodsonofabitch." Bernadine spit out the angry words into the air. "I knew he was up to something with all that sweet talk."

"What sweet talk?" I put my hand on her arm to stop her and catch my breath. "Oh no." My gut twisted and turned. "Please don't tell me you did something really stupid like. . ."

"Sleep with him?" she asked. "Yes. I slept with Henry the night of his death."

"Oh God, Bernadine! Why?" I begged and veered the way she was walking. I looked up and we were heading toward her house.

"I need a drink." She motioned for me and Willow to follow her.

"I need a drink," I repeated. "What about the Diva pact?"

"What was I supposed to do in the heat of the moment? Henry, can you stop telling me how much you messed up and you have come back because you missed me and life can't go on without me, so I can call my divorced girlfriends so they can talk me out of getting my old life back?" She stopped midway up to her house and looked at me.

"Yes." I nodded my head. "The pact was so we could put a little air between the conversations our exes put in our heads to second guess ourselves. We wouldn't have talked you out of anything. It would have made you pause."

"He has such amazing hands." Bernadine's face set with worry. "That's what made him such a good dentist. And his eyes." She put her hands on her heart and let out a big sigh. "One look into them and he knows he has me undressed."

"Bernadine." I gulped. I couldn't believe that I was about to ask her this. "Did you have anything to do with Henry's death?" I put my hands out. "If you did, we can get through this."

The evidence was against her. The knife was from her house. Was it a fit of passion? Did they fight after they had sex and she took the knife and stabbed him? Did she

accidentally take the crimp tool from the Wine and Bead class?

"Hell no!" Bernadine balled up her fists and walked around her house. I trailed behind, tugging Willow up the hill.

Weak, weak, weak. Willow whined all the way up the hill. Bernadine was already in the front of the house.

"Come on, girl." I encouraged her to keep going, but with every step her snout was seeking something in the grass.

I tugged harder bringing her a few more steps. I yanked more. She held her ground. Her snout was digging under a big rock.

"No. You aren't eating bugs!" I yelled and pulled her more. She refused, jerking me forward.

Groink, groink, groink. Willow's leash was pulled tight.

So not to bruise her neck, I went over and kicked the rock to get it out of her reach. The sunlight exposed all sorts of bugs that lived in the cold dark under. Something shiny caught my eye. I used the toe of my shoe to move some of the bugs that Willow hadn't already scarfed up out of the way to see what the shiny thing was.

"Strange." I bent down and picked up the small square metal piece with a metal tooth sticking up out of the middle. It didn't seem like something I would want, but I have learned to never leave any stone unturned in a murder case. Literally.

I stuck it in my pocket and yanked on Willow. When we finally made it around to the front, I found Bernadine on the long covered porch that spanned the entire front of her house. She was slowly rocking in the rocking chair sipping on pink lemonade.

"I truly can't believe you asked me if I killed Henry!" She looked past me and out over the road. "Of all the Divas, I thought you were the one who always believed in me. Were they lies? Do you really not think I can lose weight? What about Second Cup? You encouraged me to open it."

I tied Willow's leash to the post. She had found some more bugs to snack on in Bernadine's landscape. I stomped up the steps.

"Of course I believe in you." I sat in the chair next to hers. "But you broke the Diva code and now he's dead. I'm not saying you did it, but now it's going to be awfully suspicious."

I fidgeted with my pants. Something was stabbing me in the thigh. I put my hand in the front pocket and pulled out the little metal piece I had found by the rock in her side yard.

"I was just saying that if you did harm him," I was careful not to use the word murdered, "that we could get through this."

"Well I didn't." There was anger in her eyes. "He told me there was no one else. And you are telling me that there are at least two."

"Why did you sleep with him when he was suing you to stop alimony?" I asked.

It seemed like he was trying to butter her up.

"He said that if we got back together he would be paying for everything anyway." A tear fell out of her eyes. "Deep down I knew he was trying to sweet talk me. But for one minute I wanted to believe that he still wanted me. Wanted all of me. Not just the money I was taking from him."

Get back together? How could she fall for that line? Didn't we all want to hear that from our exes at one time or another?

"Fine." I could relate to what she was saying. Just a few short months ago before I had Donovan, I would have given anything to be back in Sean's bed. "Let's go over the time frame of that night. Maybe we can come up with something."

Bernadine stood up and I followed her inside.

"Do you know what this is?" I held the metal piece in the palm of my hand.

Bernadine picked it up and without a beat knew exactly what it was.

"It's the metal piece on the dental floss box that cuts the string." She put it back in my hand. "They slip off and on so easy."

"Do you have any of Henry's from his new office?" I asked so I could compare.

"I have a ton." She got up and walked back into the house to get it. "Henry is always carrying them."

I shrugged and put it back in my pocket. The metal piece was definitely not a piece of evidence, especially if he was here the night he was murdered.

"See." She held out the floss box that had Henry's dental logo on it. "Only Henry's is the single cut and the one you have has two."

I looked at it, but nothing stood out.

"Let's write down the timeline of events you had with Henry before he was killed so when we meet with the Divas tonight, we can collectively put our heads together." There had to be something we were missing. "We need to give each Diva a job. Something to help."

Chapter Twelve

After Bernadine and I wrote down the events the night of Henry's death when she was with him, I walked Willow home and grabbed a few items. She and I had to get to the shop for the long night ahead of us.

I had a bridal consultation with a bride I had already put a few items together for before the impromptu Diva meeting. And I still hadn't called Donovan to let him know I wouldn't be at the self-defense class.

Before Marlene even opened her mouth, Willow scrambled through the storage room door. Marlene didn't pay any attention to Willow. She hoisted the sleeves of her knit shirt up to her elbows and crossed her arms across her chest, making the scoop neckline expose more cleavage than she should.

"You're late." Marlene snarled and tapped her acrylic nail on her watch. "The bride is not happy."

We both turned our heads in the direction of the bride's table. The young woman was seated and the mother was standing next to her rubbing her neck.

When I got married to Sean, there wasn't anyone standing next to the me and him but the judge. There was something wrong with all of these girls. Each one trying to outdo the other.

"This one is a Bridezilla." Marlene chomped. Her gum popped with each word. "She's all yours."

All mine. I sighed.

"I'm sorry." The five-foot-four-inch bride bolted over to me. "Did *I* have the time wrong? Or did *you* forget about me?"

"Sarah, I'm sorry. Another bride fitting took a little longer than I had planned. But I'm here now." I clasped my hands together and planted a smile on my face.

"This is *my* wedding. I don't care about any other brides." Her green eyes glared at me. Her freckles across her nose reddened.

"Dear, Holly is here now." Sarah's mom put her hand on Sarah's arm.

Sarah jerked away. Her eyes slid from me, to her mom and back to me.

"If it weren't for Margaret McGee using you, I wouldn't be here." She ran her hands through her short brown hair in frustration. "I'd be at Diamond Lil picking out the real stuff, not these two cent fakes you have Dolly Parton over there showing me."

"I beg. . ." Marlene stomped her way over when she heard Sarah putting her down.

"There is no need to yell at Marlene just because you are mad at me. I promise you will walk down the aisle wearing a beautiful design that you have created that no one else in the world will ever have." I did a lot of sweet talking and backpedaling. Sarah was the biggest client I'd had since Margaret. "When you saw Margaret's beautiful crystal set, did you fall in love with it? Did you want it? Did you want something better than it?"

"Yes," Sarah gasped. A big grin crossed her perfectly stained white teeth. "Yes."

"Here I am. Just like I was here for Margaret. Let's get to work and create the designs everyone at your wedding will be talking about." Gracefully, I took Sarah by the elbow and guided her toward the table.

As if Marlene knew what I was saying, she rushed to the back room and fetched a chilled bottle of champagne and a few cheese squares and Triscuits.

"Are these low-fat?" Sarah asked with her big green doe-eyes staring up at Marlene.

"Of course they are." Marlene planted a shit-eating grin on her face.

We both knew they were not low fat, but we weren't about to spoil Sarah's dream.

"Here we have a beautiful fifteen by ten centimeter briolette in grey. These are exquisite, sought-after gems." I held the grey stone in the air toward the sun to show Sarah and her mother the brilliance of the stone.

I brought the stone back down and placed it on the bead board. I had a plastic box, sort of like a small tackle box, with Sarah's name on a tag and attached to the handle.

"Here is your bride box." I opened it and a display of beautiful stones I had handpicked for her were in neat little compartments.

"Since you are having a mix of lovely yellow and grey bridesmaid dresses, these briolette teardrops will make a stunning wrap necklace with a dash of graduated rounds in a pale yellow to compliment the drops." I took out the different beads I was talking about and placed them neatly on the bead board, carefully laying out the design as I talked.

Like a magnificent, one of a kind painting, the necklace came together, creating a masterpiece that lit Sarah up like she had just won the Miss Universe pageant.

"Oh, Momma!" She gasped.

Delicately, she reached out her perfectly manicured nude nails and quickly retracted them before she even touched the design as if she wasn't good enough to touch it.

"It's going to be amazing, Holly." She put her hands to her mouth. A line of water sat at the edge of her lids. She took a deep breath and got herself together. "I'm going to need fifteen sets."

"Sets?" My jaw dropped.

There was no way I was going to be able to afford the stones to make fifteen of these necklaces without using my credit card, much less fifteen sets which included earrings and a bracelet.

"Is there a problem?" Bridezilla was back. She'd quickly forgotten how happy I had just made her with my impromptu designs.

"There is not a problem one." Marlene chimed from the counter where she was pulling pre-made jewelry out of the glass cabinet for a lingering customer.

"Right." I snapped my fingers. "No problem."

The dingy bell above the door jingled.

"Now there is a problem," I muttered when I looked to see who walked in.

Officer Beverly Kiss.

"Good afternoon." Officer Kiss rested her hands on her holster.

If I had the nerve, I might have asked her where she would place her hands if her holster wasn't there because every time I had seen her in her uniform, that was where she had them.

"I'll be with you in a minute," I said and turned back to Sarah who happened to be picking through her bridal box.

"Our next appointment is scheduled in a couple days, right?" Sarah asked. She picked up one bead after the other and held them up to the sun.

"I have all the appointments listed on your tag attached to your bride's box." I gestured to the lid.

I had found it had been easier to schedule the appointments in advance to not only keep me on schedule, but it also put the brides a little more at ease. There were four different scheduled appointments after the initial meeting. Each one was used to perfect the design and if more were needed, there was allotted time toward the end.

"At that appointment, we will work on the final design of the most important piece." I paused for a dramatic effect. "Yours."

A secretive smile formed on Sarah's lips as though she was holding the biggest piece of classified information for brides.

"All my own?" she questioned. "No one else in the world will have my design."

I nodded. "One of a kind," I said again nailing the coffin shut.

It was a shame that all of Margaret's friends were coming in here telling me that they all wanted to one up her and the other girls. I couldn't imagine the Divas all trying to backstab each other.

Ahem. Officer Kiss cleared her throat.

"I have to go now." I closed Sarah's bride box and picked it up. "I'll see you in a couple days."

Sarah didn't say a word to apologize for her behavior. Not a thank you or sorry I was so rude, which I wished she had done. And her mother didn't even correct her. Her mom followed right behind her as they waltzed right out of the store.

"Can I see that?" Officer Kiss pointed to Sarah's bridal box that was under my arm.

"Why?" I asked and squeezed my arm a little closer to my body.

There wasn't a real reason she couldn't look in it, but it was at least one thing that the police didn't have access to. Plus I wanted to know why.

"Do you do those for all the brides?" Her eyes were sharp and assessing.

"Fine." I said.

I would like to say that I resigned to her request so I could get some clues, but truth-be-told, I didn't look good in orange and that was the color of Swanee's detention center jumpsuits.

I put the box on the table and opened it.

"These are bridal boxes for each bride that contracts me to design some sort of jewelry for their wedding." I pointed to the tag. "Every one has the bride's name attached to it and on the other side of the tag are all the appointments we had scheduled for the project."

Officer Kiss had a little notebook like Noah. I wondered if those were distributed in their cop classes or whatever they took. Or if there was a secret cop store where they picked up their little notebooks.

She was always a pretty gal. Her long brown hair was all one length. When she was on the job she wore it up in a loose ponytail bun on the back of her head. The blue uniform did bring out her blue eyes against her olive skin. She had nice, thick eyebrows that were shaped perfectly to fit her eyes. Her police radio was clipped on the left shoulder; her badge was pinned above the pocket over her heart from which she retrieved that notebook. On each side of the shirt, a little below the shoulder, there was a small pin with the initials S.P.D. I could only assume stood for Swanee Police Department.

Her upper body was a little puffed out due to the bulletproof vest, which led to a much smaller waist that was cinched with the belt full of all the cop paraphernalia. My eyes glazed over the gun, Taser, flashlight, handcuffs and all the other stuff she had stuck on there.

Sadly, she still looked thinner than me and I only had on a thin layer of clothing.

"Okay." She pointed her pen at the bride box for me to continue.

"Oh," I shook my head to get back into the game. "It's the same as a tackle box. All of these different compartments holds a different example of beads I collected after my initial sit down with the bride-to-be, where she fills out a form that has the type of wedding she is having along with the colors she would like."

"Kind of wedding?" She cocked her brow as a little laugh escaped her lips.

"Outside, inside, fancy, or not." I waved my hands in the air. "Shit, Sean and I got married in front of the Justice of the Peace. I don't think I had any jewelry on."

"What about under here?" She pointed to the tray that lifted off.

"Under," I whispered.

Though I knew what was under there, sweat beaded up on my palms as I lifted the tray. Deep down I knew nothing was going to jump out or grab me, but *you never know* always sat in the back of my head. A very poisonous spider could've gotten in there and it could possibly jump out and bite me.

I picked up the tray and placed it on the table next to the box. Officer Hart leaned over. She blew a stray hair that fell into her face, almost making her seem a little more personable.

"Do you always keep these types of things in the bottom?" she asked referring to the tools and stringing equipment.

"Yes." I peeked over her shoulder. "Sometimes I have to meet the bride the day of the wedding or during a rehearsal, so I grab their box and go."

"What about these?" She picked up the crimping tool.

"Everything you see in there is what I use." I held up a finger. "If I have made all the pieces, I will take out the tray and put the finished product in there because I obviously don't need the beads anymore."

"What about the tools? Do you take those out?" she asked, replacing the crimp tool and picking up the pliers.

"No," I said and shook my head. "Every tool in there is a must and can be used at anytime."

"How so?"

"If I'm at the church before the wedding and say the bracelet breaks, which I have never had happen," I said and knocked on my head to gesture as wood. "These are the only tools I need to repair the bracelet within minutes."

"I see." She sat the pliers back in the box and scribbled something down on her paper. "And you keep the boxes in your possession at all times, including the weddings?"

"Yes. Umm." I thought for a second. "Not all times. Sometimes I go and watch the wedding. I collect it when the wedding is over."

"Then you bring it back here and inventory it?" She continuously wrote.

"Yes. Um. . ." I knew she was looking for details and I couldn't figure out why. "No. Sort of."

Without lifting her face up, she slid her eyes up to me with her brows lifted and she stopped writing.

"I mean, I bring it back and Marlene cleans out the boxes. She takes out the beads we didn't use, cuts off the bride's tags, cleans them with wipes, and cleans off the tools. Then she puts a new tag on it, puts the tools back in and sticks it on the shelf until we get a new client."

"How many boxes do you have?"

"Four."

"And where is the inventory list for the brides and the boxes?" she asked.

"Inventory list?" I had never heard of an inventory list for my made-up boxes. "The only inventory list I'm required to keep is the one for my accountant."

"You don't check the tools back in as you get them out? So anyone could take your tools and you'd never know?" she asked.

I didn't like her tone. I could see where this was going.

"What are you saying?" I asked straightforward.

"Your tool was found at Dr. Frisk's dental office. There are no prints on it other than his and some of his blood." She put her hand flat on the table and leaned so close to me I could tell she was chewing Zebra Stripes tutti-fruity gum. "Someone either came in here and took a tool from underneath your nose during one of your beading classes, though you claim you count those every time." She stood up, ramrod straight with her arms across her chest. "Or someone took them from a bride's box when you weren't looking."

Damn. She was good.

Unfortunately, I knew there was a pair missing from the other night and it was around Bernadine's chair, which made me shudder to think it could have been Bernadine. But she did sleep with him and he did tell her that he still wanted to sue her even though he was trying to give her the pack of lies about getting back together and taking care of her.

"I'm going to need that bride inventory list." Officer Hart didn't budge from her spot.

My head swirled and the room began to spin. I put my hand on the table to steady myself. There was no way there was a killer in my bead shop. Or a client for that matter. Everyone was eager to learn and the brides didn't know Henry.

"Henry just moved back a few months ago." I lowered myself into one of the beading chairs. "I haven't had a wedding deadline it the past few months."

"This could have been a premeditated murder."

"Premeditated?" That word didn't set well in my gut.

"That means that someone had this planned."

"I know what it means." I couldn't help but be a little proud that my crime TV knowledge was helping out a little bit. "But who would've known that Henry Frisk was coming back?"

"Maybe they didn't. But maybe Henry Frisk pissed that person off and that person wanted to kill him." She sucked in a deep breath. "I'm not saying this is right, but the someone that wanted to kill him is doing a great job pointing the evidence to Bernadine."

"Bernadine didn't do this." I assured her.

"Women who are angry can get tempers, Holly." Her eyes lowered. "You know that."

She was good at reminding me about all the times the police were called to help settle a fight between me and Sean any given weekend night in which we had a little too much liquid courage from The Livin' End.

"I do, but Bernadine had no reason to hurt him, much less kill him." I slumped down in my chair.

"I think when your lifestyle is about to change that puts a great deal of stress on a woman, don't you?" she snidely asked.

"Yes. I had a hard time when Sean left me and yes I did have to borrow money from Ginger, but I'm not Bernadine." It was no secret that I had a hard time making ends meet when Sean left me and Willow high and dry. We had to find a place to live and I had to get a job. That was when I moved into Ginger's country lake cottage and opened The Beaded Dragonfly. "As you can see, I've made it on my own. And Bernadine has too with Second Cup."

"And if what you say is true, then someone has stolen your tools to pin the murder on her along with her great motive." Officer Hart tapped the end of her pen on her notebook. "What about that inventory list of brides."

"Marlene," I stood up and walked over to the counter. Marlene was doing a good job pretending she was shining the glass beads when she was actually all ears.

"I don't keep a log," She leaned over the counter and whispered. "I just take out the beads and never really pick up the tray because there is always so much left over."

"Did you say that you don't keep a log of when the bride boxes are returned?" Office Hart didn't look up as she wrote.

"Not in those words, but yes." Marlene let out a long sigh. "I clip off the bride's tag and put a new one on. I take out the left over beads and put them back in stock. Then I put the box back on the shelf."

"So. . ." Officer Hart hesitated. "You have no idea when someone took the crimp tool. Actually, stole the crimp tool, which is a crime in itself. Interesting."

Marlene and I stood there and watched Officer Hart walk out of the shop. We waited in silence before we saw her get into her police car and pull out.

"Holly." Marlene's voice was shaky. "Weren't you looking for a crimp tool after the Wine and Bead class?"

"Yes." I tried to swallow the lump in the middle of my throat.

"Did I notice you looking around for it where Bernadine was sitting?" She sounded like she was almost afraid to hear my answer.

"Yes," I murmured under my breath.

"Do you think—"

"I don't know," I interrupted her before I let the words escape her mouth.

The evidence was mounting up. Bernadine was not happy with Henry. Who would be? He was trying to stop her alimony. She was a Diva and we did dream up bad ways to hurt our exes, but never *kill them*. That would let them off too easy.

Bernadine's crimp tool was missing from the Wine and Bead class. They found the crimp tool in his office. And she's missing the exact same knife Noah Druck claimed was the actual murder weapon.

As much as I didn't want to believe Bernadine didn't do it, Officer Hart's words replayed over and over. *"I think when your lifestyle is about to change that puts a great deal of stress on a woman, don't you?"*

"Marlene!" Bernadine used her butt to swing open the bead shop door. The bells jingled. She held her arms in the air, a bottle of wine in each. "Grab the glasses. It's wine o'clock and I'm drinking a few glasses."

Chapter Thirteen

"Noah Druck showed up right after you left with a warrant to look for the knife set." Bernadine wrapped her fingers around her wine glass. She lifted the glass to her lips and took a big gulp. "He was a little too late." She winked.

"What does that mean?" I asked her.

The Divas trickled in one-by-one for the impromptu meeting interrupting my conversation with Bernadine. The wink wasn't a friendly wink. It was the kind that told me she took care of something. What was that something?

"Bernadine," Cheri rushed over to Bernadine's side. Her black hair was neatly tucked up in a teal crocheted beret. "How are you?"

"Someone is definitely trying to frame me for the murder of Henry and I have no idea who it is or why they are doing it." The edges of her eyes dipped into a frown.

I watched her body language closely as Ginger, Agnes, and Flora got caught up on the gossip of what was going on with the investigation. She told them about the crimp tool and the knife, but failed to tell them that she had a matching set of knives minus that particular knife. I kept my mouth shut.

"It's my understanding that Bradford was at The Livin' End the night Henry was on a date with some blond girl." It was a good time to get the Divas involved in the investigation. Bernadine was a Diva and I was going to have to put any doubts aside and try to help figure out who really did kill Henry.

"Date?" Agnes Pearl picked at the grey hair that curled in the middle of her ear. "Henry was dating?"

All eyes slid to Bernadine.

"I thought he was dating me." Her voice lowered along with her head. She twirled her fingers in her lap as silence fell over the group. "Apparently, Henry was trying to sweet talk me into signing the papers to discontinue the alimony money by telling me how much he missed me and wanted to get back together. And he got me back in bed just hours before someone killed him."

Something then happened that never happened. The Divas were speechless. I'm not even sure if any of them were breathing.

"That bastard!" Marlene yelled out snapping everyone to the present.

"Bastard," Agnes Pearl whispered and shook her head.

"Did you tell Bennie about that?" Flora hen-pecked on her phone. We all knew she was sending Bennie a message. "Any of them two-bit women could have killed him."

"Why?" Bernadine asked.

"Maybe he told one of them that he was going to get back together with you?" Cheri smacked her hand on the table. We all grabbed our wine glasses to save them from tipping over.

"Yeah, yeah." Marlene chomped. "What if he was serious about getting back together and he met the blonde to tell her that he was getting back together with you?"

There was a little glimmer of hope in Bernadine's eyes. I could tell she was wanting so bad to think Henry was regretting all he had done to her, but deep down we all knew he wasn't.

"Agnes, do you think you could have Bradford over for a little lunch or dinner and pick his brain?" I asked.

"I do owe him a batch of fudge for getting me out of my ticket." Agnes said.

We all kept our lips pinched. Agnes was always causing some sort of trouble and Bradford spent most of his time trying to get her out.

"That would be great, Agnes," Bernadine said and fiddled with the zipper on her jacket.

Willow's hooves sounded like high-heels trotting out of the storage room. She could hear Bernadine's snack baggie from miles away. I glanced up at the clock. We had been here for almost forty minutes and nothing was getting accomplished.

The facts still remained. All the evidence in the murder pointed to Bernadine.

There were people there that I needed to question about Dr. Russell and Henry's fight. Cheri had a plausible suspect with the other women, but Dr. Russell had more to lose than anyone. . .his livelihood.

"I'm still thinking we need to look into Dr. Russell's fight with Henry." I tapped my watch. "That is why I am going to the Barn Dance Committee meeting tomorrow night at seven."

"You?" Flora's mouth dropped. "I thought you and Bobbi Hart had a little spat about that."

"Spit-spat." I blew it off. "It's time I started to really become part of this community."

"Holly Harper, I know you better than that." Agnes Pearl's eyelashes lowered sending a shadow down her cheeks, calling me out on my downright lie.

"Fine. I had to eat a big piece of humble pie and give her a free stretchy bracelet." I smiled from ear-to-ear. I looked at Bernadine. "Anything for my Divas."

"So I'm going to have Bradford over for fudge. Cheri you are. . ." Agnes was assigning tasks. "You. . ."

"I will go get my teeth cleaned from Dr. Russell and tell him that I had an appointment with Henry to get a cavity filled." She shrugged. "And since he is dead, I had to come to him."

"Where do you normally go?" Flora asked adjusting her phone between her shoulder and ear.

"I haven't been to the dentist in years." Cheri showed her teeth that were perfectly white and straight. "I'm sure I don't have a cavity, but he doesn't know that. I can tell him about my fake visit to Henry and see if I can get him all riled up and want to talk to me."

"Holly, you are going to find out about the fight between Dr. Russell and Henry." Agnes pointed her crooked finger toward Flora. "What are you going to do?"

"Me?" Flora jerked back. Phone was still in her hand. "I gave you Bennie. He is the glue holding this shit together." She twirled her finger around.

All of us jumped when there was a knock at the door. Bernadine's baggie of carrots flew in the air. Willow scrambled to eat them all up.

"Charlie, what are you doing here?" I asked when I opened the door to find her standing on the bead shop steps. She was crazy if she thought I was going to forgive her for being so mean and rude.

"I'm here to drop these off to Bernadine for Barbie." She held the tray of low-fat goodies in the air for Bernadine to see. "Sadie said you were down here for a bead meeting."

Charlie didn't bother to wait for me to step aside. She stepped high-heel right on over me like a long-legged giraffe. I couldn't help but notice the Swarovski crystal toggle bracelet on her wrist.

Snort, snort, snort. Half of Willow's body was stuck in the *Under* of the sterling silver bead shelf.

"Barbie told me to have you try this one." Charlie handed Bernadine the specially wrapped muffin. Marlene reached over to get a pinch. Charlie smacked her hand away. I couldn't take my eyes off of Charlie's wrist. "That is specifically for Bernadine. If you want one, you can buy one at Second Cup in the morning."

"You little. . ." Marlene spit between gritted teeth.

"Charlie," I interrupted before Marlene did to Charlie what someone had done to Henry. I ignored Willow. She was distracted by a stray carrot. "Where did you get that bracelet?"

"I made it." She ran her hands over top of it almost hiding it from me.

"Where?" I asked out of curiosity.

"My house."

Her house?

"Nice." There weren't any noticeable flaws, which made me wonder if she was really a novice beader as she had acted like in the Wine and Bead class.

"Thank you, Holly." She sat the plate of treats next to Bernadine. "Barbie hopes they sell. I would love to hang around, but I'm meeting Sean for a drink." She winked and turned to strut out the door. "And who knows what the night will bring." She shrugged.

“Don’t pay her any attention, Holly.” Flora said when the door closed right behind Charlie. “She can have your sloppy seconds.”

“Yeah. Sloppy seconds,” Agnes repeated with a chuckle. “She sure does have a nice body though.”

“Why didn’t you let me at her?” Marlene pumped her fists in the air. “I’d show that blonde bimbo a thing or two.”

“OHMYGOD!” I jumped in the air. My adrenaline was pumping. My mind was reeling. “Blonde. Bracelet.”

I was putting two-and-two together.

“What, Holly?” the Divas said in unison.

Weak, weak, weak. Willow cried.

“Henry remodeled the old building and used Buskin Design. Charlie is an interior decorator for Buskins. She’s blonde. Henry was with a blonde at The Livin’ End.” I smacked my hands together. “And she can’t make a toggle bracelet without a crimping tool and she was here the night of the Wine and Bead!”

Weak, weak, weak.

"Stop, Willow!" I screamed.

Cheri rushed over to see what Willow was wanting in the *Under*.

"Umm, Holly." Cheri stood back up. She held up a pair of crimp tools in her fingers. "And I don't think you are missing any crimp tools either."

"My missing tool!" There wasn't anything that made me happier than to see that tool.

Bernadine really didn't kill Henry.

"You might be right." Bernadine's hands were over her mouth. "But how are we going to find out?"

"Henry kept a log of every single meeting he had. Even dates he planned with me when we were married. Very, very structured life he led. One of our downfalls. " She reached into her purse and pulled out her key ring full of keys. "I have the spare to Henry's office and I bet his calendar is there somewhere. If he had a date with Charlie, it would be in there. Or his phone."

"Phone?" I asked.

"Yes. He loves to film himself after each patient to dictate. It's weird but it works. Or he will write something down and take a photo of it if he can't dictate at the time. Strange, but it works for him."

"Great! I will look for the calendar and the phone. It looks like me and you are going to Henry Frisk's office." I swallowed hard and pointed to Bernadine. "Charlie is also redoing Dr. Russell's office. I can't help but wonder if she and Dr. Russell had something to do with Henry's murder."

"No way am I going anywhere near there." Bernadine shook her head. "If I go there and Noah finds out, he will pull the *you are the one who went back to the scene of the crime* stuff you see on TV."

"We need to get in that office." I knew that there had to be some sort of clue somewhere. The calendar. Something.

"Don't you think that Noah and she-officer have combed the place and taken out everything they possibly could find?" Flora wasn't a fan of Officer Kiss either.

“Maybe.” I shrugged. “But we have to try. And you can go with me.”

“Me? But I gave you . . .”

“Zip it and come on.” I grabbed by bag and keys. “Marlene, can you close up? Cheri can you take Willow for a quick walk? And Bernadine.” I turned to look at her. She looked up. Her eyes were hollow. There was the unspoken knowledge of the knife between us. “Can you take Willow home for me? And I’ll call you in the morning?”

Chapter Fourteen

Flora moaned all the way to Henry Frisk's dental office.

"Flora, we have to help Bernadine out." I reminded her of how we stick together.

I pulled down the street on the far edge of town where Henry had bought an old Victorian House that had been vacant for years. As part of the revitalization of Swanee, the old house was one of many that sold on the courthouse steps in an auction. Too bad they weren't doing that when I opened The Beaded Dragonfly.

"I know that." Flora tapped her finger on her phone. "But can't Ernie do this? I just don't want to be caught doing anything we aren't supposed to do."

"That didn't stop you when you murdered Bennie's clothes after he left you." I reminded her about her little run-in with Noah Druck and how the entire town found out about the Divorced Divas.

"Plus," she paused, "I'm not so sure Bernadine is innocent."

"How could you say that?" I drove slowly past the dental office. There was still police tape strung all over, which meant it was still considered a crime scene and no one other than authorized personnel was admitted. The place was dark. Scary.

At the end of the street, I made a U-turn and headed back toward the dental office.

"Bennie said that the knife that was weapon came from Bernadine's house," she said in a low voice as if she didn't want to say it out loud.

"How do they know that?" I asked.

"Noah Druck told Bennie that he needs to get Bernadine to confess because they went back through her credit card statements and she had purchased an exact matching set of knives from a fancy store up in Lexington. One of those kitchen stores." She bit her lip and looked out the windshield with her hands folded in her lap.

"Then anyone could have those knives." There wasn't any way I was going to give up that easy.

"I'm not saying there aren't." She shifted her body toward me. "But the coincidence is pretty far-fetched."

"Did Bennie ask her about it?" I flipped the lights off the Beetle when I assessed there were no cops cars or anyone else for that matter at the crime scene.

"No. He was going to drive over to her house after our Diva meeting." She held up her phone. "That was who I was talking to at The Beaded Dragonfly. He wanted me to let him know when we were going to be finished. That was when he told me about the knife."

I pulled the car over a few houses down from Henry's office and turned the car off. I put my hand on the gearshift between our seats.

"It's not looking good, Holly." She put her hand on mine. "Unfortunately, women do things that we think they aren't capable of in the heat of passion. Especially since she and Henry had just made love. It is all making sense to me now."

Everything Flora was saying made so much sense, but I just couldn't take that for what it was worth. I had to find out for myself. There were too many things about Dr. Russell and Charlie that set off my alarms.

"Okay. I will give you that it isn't looking good. But we are here and I want to see for myself." I pulled my hand out from under hers and took the keys out of the ignition. "You don't have to go with me if you don't want. But you have to keep watch and let me know if you see anyone coming."

"I can do that." She nodded.

Without another word between us, I held my keys in my fist just like Donovan had taught me to do.

Donovan. Shit.

I looked down at my phone. It was almost eight p.m. and he would already be in the self-defense class getting ready to teach. I had completely forgotten to call him. Somehow I would make it up to him after all of this was over.

Quickly I ran behind the house next to the office. A security light popped on. I hid in the shadow hoping no one saw it and if they did, I prayed they thought it was a cat darting around.

After waiting a few seconds, though it seemed like minutes, I tiptoed over to the office. The thought of a dead body there made my skin crawl.

I decided to stay around the back in the shadows of the night. I looked around to see if I could see any video equipment like Ginger was looking in on, but I didn't see any. Nor did I see any large security lights that Henry might have installed himself.

The gingerbread lattice around the wrap around porch was beautiful. Henry had done a really nice job restoring the old Victorian and I could only imagine what kind of taste Charlie had. She had great taste when it came to her appearance; I could only imagine the pride she had in decorating for the world to see.

She was going to have her hands full with Dr. Russell's old office.

I slipped under the police tape and darted up the steps. I looked left and right, trying to take shallow breaths and keep my cool. My hands were shaking.

"Calm down," I whispered and held my hand out in front of me so I could put it on the door handle. I took another deep breath and just went for it. I had the door handle in my hand and turned.

Nothing.

What in the world did I think was going to happen? Did I honestly think that the door wasn't locked? Did I totally act like the police tape wasn't strung all around me? So there was no other choice but to use Bernadine's key, which made me a little nervous because I felt like that was sort of falling under the umbrella of breaking and entering. I wasn't necessarily breaking anything, but I was illegally entering a crime scene that still seemed to be active.

"What am I doing?" I asked myself and fumbled the key around the key hole.

All I had to do was think of that bloody knife and how Noah knew it had come from Bernadine's house. But how did it get into the hands of the killer?

The office smelled just like a dentist office, which surprised me. The idea of having an interior decorator made me think it would somehow disguise the smell that so many have come to fear. With the sick feeling of being at the dentist and the idea that there was a murder in the exact same place, I began to feel woozy.

I pulled the collar of my shirt up over my nose and took a deep breath. Secret deodorant was a far better smell than . . .death.

"Eeck!" I screamed when I looked down and noticed a spot had been cut out of the carpet in the reception area. A spot big enough for one dead Henry Frisk.

I used the flashlight feature on my cell to get a better look. It was definitely a cut out of what looked to be the place Henry was stabbed. The exposed subflooring had a large dark spot that I could only assume was the blood that had seeped through the carpet and foam.

My eyes followed the flashlight beam to the cushioned chairs and walls which had numbers written beside them along with some police tape marking the blood splatter. It looked like the murderer might have hit one of Henry's main arteries and as his heart pumped, the blood shot out onto the walls and chairs.

At that moment, I was thankful Bernadine wasn't with me. By the looks of the crime scene, there was no way she could've done this. She wouldn't be able to get any part of her outfit dirty. Whoever did this, had to have blood somewhere on their clothes.

Obviously, Noah Druck didn't know Bernadine very well. . .at all.

I used the flashlight to do a little more looking around, careful not to touch anything. Like Bernadine, the last thing Noah needed was more ammunition to use against another Diva. Then he'd have a field day trying to bring our whole group down.

The artwork on the walls was definitely not like any doctor's office I had ever seen. They were very contemporary pieces with lots of colors. Even the walls were a bright yellow.

I peeked my head into one of the dental cleaning rooms. The chairs were modern. I stepped in to get a closer look and couldn't help myself.

"Ahh." I laid back and used the electronic keypad on the arm of the chair to give me the massage treatment Ginger said she had gotten. The feeling of having to go pee-pee hit me. "Not a good time to have to go," I said and opened my eyes.

Temporarily, I had forgotten why I was there and quickly jumped up. I plucked a couple of Kleenex from the counter and tried to wipe off any prints before I rushed out of there and down to Henry's office.

The office was also modern with a glass desk and chair that was neatly tucked underneath it. He had several *Unders* in there and there was no way in hell I was going to stick my hand in the depths of the dark. But I had a flashlight.

I did a little pee-pee dance and wiggled my way down to the floor. With my butt stuck up in the air, I peered underneath the first *Under* and pointed the cell flashlight. Nothing but dust bunnies so I went down the line doing my routine until I reached the last *Under* where a little flutter of something caught my eye.

A feather. A brown and white feather with a red tip.

Carefully I stuck my hand and pulled it out, keeping the flashlight on it the whole time. Not that a feather was a big deal, but it seemed like a big deal to me.

Now, if I were in my house, there are feathers all over from my feather pillow. I had no idea how those darn things got out of the pillow, but they did and they were everywhere I turned. Lucky for me, there were no *Unders* in my house, so I sucked them up in the vacuum.

I didn't see any throw pillows and I knew Henry wasn't farting feathers. I tucked it down in my pocket and got up to find the calendar Bernadine insisted Henry had and his phone.

The desk was as clean as a whistle with only a laptop on it. The darn thing was covered in what looked like to be fingerprinting powder, which Noah was good at using liberally. That meant that they had already gone through the files on the computer so I didn't waste my time. And I bet they had already gotten Henry's phone and phone records. That was probably the first thing Noah had done or gotten off Henry's body.

There weren't any drawers on the desk. Just a couple of sawhorses holding up a large piece of thick glass. Very modern. Very Charlie.

With the tissues still in my hand, I started to open up all the fancy furniture drawers, but nothing was in them. If he did have a calendar, it looked like Noah had beaten us to it.

Ding. My phone chimed a text. It was Flora wondering how much longer because she was a little scared.

Now seemed like a good time since there was nothing there. Not even the carpet. I made my way down the dark hall and nearly passed out when my shin hit something in the dark. I used the light on my phone to see what it was. A fire extinguisher.

"Damn." I rubbed my shin when the pain wasn't going away.

I passed the bathroom on my way out the way I had come in and decided to slip on in there. I had to turn on the light to see and I used my shoe to shut the door, but not completely. I figured the bathroom was in the far part of the office and no one would be able to see the light, especially with the door partially closed. Hopefully Noah wasn't going to come back through and do a butt check on the toilet seat, but for good measure, I laid toilet paper all over it and flushed it down when I was finished.

There was never a time I hadn't washed my hands after going to the bathroom, but now seemed like the logical time to skip that step. . .only I couldn't bear to do it.

With my elbow, I turned on the handle of the faucet and quickly ran my hands under the light stream of running cold water. When I went to grab one of the fancy disposable hand towels, I noticed something sticking out

who told us about the calendar he kept. "Anyway, I have a theory about what happened."

"Okay." Flora put her hands on the dash when I took the left turn out of Henry's street to head back to The Beaded Dragonfly to drop her off at her car. "You might be great at running a business and you are definitely an awesome jewelry designer, but you are not a cop. You need to leave all this investigative stuff up to the real people like Noah."

"Flora?" I questioned her. "Since when did you turn on the opposite side of the Divas?"

"I just think we need to let Bennie see what he can do for Bernadine." She crossed her arms over her chest and stared out the passenger window.

"Oh my God! Flora!" My mouth dropped open. "You think Bernadine killed him. Don't you?"

"Like I said earlier." She continued to stare out the window. "The evidence is all mounted up against Bernadine and it makes sense."

"Henry pissed someone off in Swanee and they have pinned the evidence on Bernadine. Plain and simple." I believed it with all my heart.

"You aren't Sherlock Holmes. The facts are the facts. He was cutting her off financially. She went in there wielding her knife and slashed him up. Plain and simple." She huffed and puffed. "I'm not saying she didn't have good cause to rid that piece of shit off the face of the earth, but I'm not saying he deserved to die either. I'm sure she didn't go in there to intentionally kill him, maybe only to threaten him."

"No. I refuse to believe she could harm a fly." I couldn't believe I was actually hearing Flora say this. After all the times we Divas had stood by her and the demise of her and Bennie. "Did you forget all the times Bernadine sat in your apartment with you and held your hand when Bennie informed you that he was *gay*?"

"Crime of passion. Bennie can get her a lower sentence on crime of passion." Flora refused to see it any other way.

I stopped the car in front of the shop and put it in park.

“Please,” I begged her. “Please pretend to believe in her or don’t come around at all.”

“Holly,” Flora gasped. “You can’t say that the facts aren’t the facts. She admitted to sleeping with him right before he was killed which was after his date with the blonde.”

“Charlie. After Charlie.” I corrected her.

Flora did make sense. But that was the problem. It made too much sense. And Bernadine insisted she didn’t kill him and I happened to believe her.

Chapter Fifteen

I didn't even bother calling Donovan after I dropped Flora off. I was so mad that I just drove straight over there, in hopes he'd offer me a beer and some good insight into what Flora was thinking. It was one for all, all for one for the Divas and Flora was putting that in jeopardy.

The streets of Swanee were quiet. Chills crept up my legs and spilled over onto my arms with the thought that there was a killer out there. Waiting. Waiting to see what was going to happen to Bernadine and if the clues they planted were going to send her to jail and not them.

I sped down Donovan's street a little faster than normal. Though it was only eleven o'clock, it was still dark and creepy out.

After parking in the driveway and noticing Donovan's lights were out, I wondered if I should have called first, but quickly put it in the back of my head and got out. He was always up for a late night visit.

After I lightly tapped on the front door, and then a little louder when the night felt like it was putting its grip on me, the front porch light flipped on and the door opened. A shirtless Donovan stood with a confused look on his face. His hair was messed up. His pajama pants were perfectly positioned on his hips right below a little patch of hair on his belly, sending me into a tizzy.

"Holly." Donovan leaned on the door and put his head up against it too in a cute kind of way. "What are you doing here?"

"I thought I would pop over and tell you about the new evidence concerning Bernadine and Henry." I held the little calendar in my hand.

"It's late."

"It's eleven." I laughed and took a step closer. "I've come over way later than that."

He closed the door a little tighter around him.

"Now isn't a good time. I have to work in the morning."

I put my hand on the door and gave a little push, but he didn't let it move at all.

"I have to work too." I laughed hoping to get a positive response from him, but there was nothing.

"Good night, Holly." His eyes were blankly staring back at me.

"Wait." I put my hand on the door to stop it from completely closing. "Donovan?"

"Not now, Holly." He went to shut the door again. Again, I put my hand up. "Holly, late nights aren't convenient for me."

"Really?" I tilted my head to the side, trying to figure out the vibe that wasn't good between us.

"Yeah, really." He took a deep breath. His bicep contracted into a tight muscle as he lifted his hand and ran it through his hair. I about died then and there. "I'm not looking for a night time hook-up or a night time shoulder to lean on with you. I'm looking for a mature relationship where my partner wants to be seen with me in the daylight around anyone. Including her ex-husband who treated her like crap and still continues to make a mockery out of her."

I stood there with my mouth dropped to my feet and watched the door shut. For a second I forgot all about Bernadine, all about dead Henry, all about my ex-ass. It wasn't until I literally made a conscious effort to pick up one foot at a time did I realize exactly what had just happened.

"Oh my God!" I beat the steering wheel through my tears with my hand and realized my ex-ass was still controlling my relationships whether he meant to or not. "Oh my God!" I screamed.

My heart felt like it was about empty. Completely empty and sitting in the bottom of my shoe. I wanted to cuss out Donovan and Sean, but logically I knew it wasn't either of their faults. It was mine. Mine for not fully letting go of my life with Sean and not allowing myself to see what could be with what was standing in front of me. A kind, loving man that didn't care what I did for a living nor cared about my extra curves.

Like a lovesick crazy teenager, I grabbed my phone and dialed Donovan's number. If he didn't want to look at me, surely he'd take my call.

"Holly, please just let it go." Donovan didn't even answer with a hello.

"I'm sorry. Please," I sobbed into the phone.

I had to pull the car over because if I didn't I was going to crash. Driving through tears was worse than trying to drive through a thunderstorm.

"I can't do it anymore." Donovan's voice was tired. Quiet. "Not too long ago there was a killer after you. When we make plans, I expect them to be kept or at least a phone call telling me you can't come or that you are okay."

"But Bernadine. . ."

He cut me off. "I had to go to the shop where Cheri told me what you were up to. I thought we were. . .," he paused, "more than friends. I thought we were dating, Holly. My mistake."

"Donovan," I couldn't bring myself to confirm that we were in fact dating, "I'm so sorry. I just jump into saving my friends mode and nothing else matters."

"See. I want to matter to someone."

"It didn't come out right. You do matter. It's just. . ." I struggled to find the words. My head was all jumbled up and not making sense.

"I have to get up and teach over two hundred college students some sort of computer junk tomorrow. I'm going to bed." Donovan had the matter-of-fact voice I had come to know all too well. Only he used it when he wouldn't let me be alone in fear of my safety. This time I think it was the safety of his heart he was protecting.

"Can we talk tomorrow?" My voice quivered in fear of his answer.

Tomorrow was better than nothing.

"I'll see. That's all I can promise, Holly." Donovan's voice was thick with strength.

The line went dead. I dropped my hand in my lap, still gripping the phone. Slowly I picked up my head and looked out the windshield. I didn't realize that I had pulled over in The Livin' End's parking lot. And right up front was Sean's beat-up work truck next to a little Fiat.

I grabbed my bag and threw the phone and calendar in it before I jumped out of the car and slammed the door.

The music was blaring out of the bar when I entered.

"You have got to be kidding me," I shouted and threw my hands in the air when I saw Sean and Charlie entangled in each other's arms dancing to Elvis's *I Can't Help Falling In Love.*

I grabbed a twenty-dollar bill out of my bag and smacked it down on the bar.

"Get me a shot of tequila and I know you can override that damn jukebox." I needed a little liquid courage. I was going to tell Sean off and accuse Charlie Hot Pants of killing Henry Frisk. "I will give you the whole twenty for the shot and you put *Suspicious Minds* by Elvis on the jukebox next."

A smile crossed the bartender's face. He had seen a lot over the years between me and Sean. Sean would know it was me playing the song seeing how I played it over and over when I accused him of all sorts of stuff and it ended up being true.

I grabbed the shot glass and held it in the grip of my hand. "This is it?" I asked looking at the measly little bit of liquid.

"Darlin'," The bartender poured another one and slid it in front of me. "I don't think you can handle much more than that. You seem to be disappearing. Getting smaller and smaller every time I see you."

"Really?" I tugged on the elastic waistband of my jeans and sure enough there was enough room for me to pinch at least an inch of material.

Come to think of it, I had forgotten to eat a few times this week and when I did it was mostly from Bernadine's Ziploc baggie of veggies, which was what I was supposed to be eating anyway.

The bartender's brows lifted and he nodded his head. I picked up the shot glass and gave an air cheers to him before I slammed it down my throat, then the second one.

By the time I turned around Sean and Charlie were gone. Elvis was belting out *Suspicious Minds*. My eyes darted around the room and they were gone.

"Damn," I said through gritted teeth. They must've slipped out when I was talking to the bartender. It probably was a good thing because I really wasn't in any shape to confront anyone. Not that I was tipsy from two shots, but my heart hurt and I wasn't sure what would come flying out of my mouth.

Though the compliment from the bartender did make me feel better. I was good enough to go home, crawl in bed and meet up with Bernadine in the morning to decode Henry's calendar.

"Nice move in there." The voice in the dark startled me when I walked out of the bar.

I turned around and Sean walked out from the shadows and into the moonlight. He flashed his million-dollar smile and shook the shaggy blond hair out of his eyes.

"When are you going to get that crap cut?" I asked.

"Still harping on my hair." He laughed. "You always hated my hair." His eyes captured mine. "Tell me, Hol, what did you like about me?"

"I. . ." I stuttered, as he got closer, feeling a little dizzy. It had to be the tequila shots.

He placed his hand on the small of my back and slightly pulled me closer.

"I never once complained about you or your weight until you started harping on my appearance." His lips moved in slow motion, getting closer to my face. "Then I got tired of hearing it so I pushed back." His breath was hot on my ear as he continued to whisper. "Don't think I haven't noticed how hot you have gotten lately. Kind of like the Hol I first married. But I figured you were off limits since big bad macho man came into your life." I put my hands on his pecs and gave a little push, not much. He held tight. "Maybe I'm wrong since you played your little Elvis song."

"Great!" Someone called out from behind us.

Sean and I jumped around when we heard someone behind us.

"Donovan." I gasped and jerked away from Sean.

He stood by his running car with his hands in his pocket.

"This." He shook his head and laughed. "I was kicking myself for turning you away tonight thinking about what could be when you got a little more confidence in yourself and the idea that I would help you overcome it." He gestured toward Sean. "Overcome him." He bit the bottom of his lip as if he was holding back anger. "I see you didn't need my help after all. You seemed to have bounced back pretty good. Good luck, Holly."

"Donovan wait!" I yelled and took a step forward, only to be held back by Sean's large hand around my wrist.

"Let him go, Hol," Sean encouraged me.

Images of him and Charlie all snuggled up on the dance floor played over in my head. Donovan's taillights disappeared down the road.

I jerked my arm from Sean.

"Don't call me Hol!" I screamed. "You lost that privilege when you left me."

I ran to the Beetle and didn't look back as the tires peeled out. There wasn't any more looking back. No looking back at my life with Sean. No looking back.

Chapter Sixteen

I had definitely made a complete mess out of my love life the night before, though I could say that the crash and burn was a process in the making. In the pit of my gut, I knew that if I didn't break all ties with Sean that Donovan and I weren't going to work out. Either way, Donovan was too good of a guy for me to leave it like the way it had been left. He had walked up to something very innocent on my part.

I would like to think that it wouldn't have gone any further than Sean sweet talking me, but the way my body tingled, I wasn't one-hundred percent sure.

"Hello?" I answered my phone that lay by my bedside table all night. I kept it there in case Donovan tried to call me. He didn't.

Willow happily snored away at the bottom of my bed. Her lump-lump body almost made it impossible for me to pull the covers up when they would wiggle down to the middle of the bed.

"Well?" Bernadine asked on the other end. "Are you going to let me in or not?"

"Are you outside?" I asked.

"Been outside for ten minutes knocking," she said.

"Oh. I guess I was out of it." The last time I had looked at the clock was four a.m. and I had probably just passed out from exhaustion. "On my way."

I pulled myself out of bed. I felt nauseous just thinking about what Donovan had walked up on. His face said it all and it's something I will never be able to get out of my mind.

"Oh," Bernadine was perfectly dressed in her khaki pants and cardigan sweater, but the outfit which usually was a little loose on her was a little tighter.

I would probably be eating everything in sight if I were under as much pressure as she was, but it definitely wasn't like her to gain so much weight so fast.

"I would say that Noah caught you breaking into Henry's office by the way you look, but I would think you would have called me if that happened."

"Henry." I planted my palm on my head, noticing I still had on the clothes I had worn the day before. "Crap." I held the door open. "Come on in."

"Are you sure it's a good time?" she asked.

Before she stepped into the cottage, she looked in and her eyes darted around the room as though she were looking for something. The pitter-patter of hooves darted down the hall, carrying all of Willow as fast as they could.

"There's my little buddy." Bernadine stepped into the cottage.

Groink, groink. Willow nudged Bernadine's calf. Bernadine and I both knew what she wanted. . . food.

"I have something for you." I walked into the kitchen and grabbed Willow's leash and Henry's calendar.

Willow needed to go potty and I had to get Bernadine out of my mind as a suspect.

"I hope you can shed some light on all this chicken scratch." I handed it to her before I clipped Willow's leash to the collar.

"Holly," Bernadine flapped. "You found it!"

She jumped up. The bag of snack fell on the floor and Willow dashed around snorting up the scattered carrots.

I tugged to get her to stop, but she was just a little too mighty.

"You are going to have to stop losing so much weight." Bernadine shot me a look before she began to thumb through the calendar. I pulled on Willow's leash, her hooves skidding across the floor in defiance, but I won.

The day was already taking shape with the bright and warm sunshine beating over the lake.

"Henry's handwriting has gotten worse over the years." Bernadine walked outside and stood on the door stoop. "Before we dig into this and you tell me exactly how you and Flora got this, tell me what's going on with you?"

Willow pulled me around every single bush that lined the front of the cottage, smelling, sniffing and snorting whatever she could.

"It wasn't real late when Flora and I got finished." I pulled a little more, but Willow was persistent on walking over to the unattached garage. "Flora made me mad so I went to see Donovan."

"Why did Flora make you mad?" Bernadine asked.

"Did I say that?" I clenched my jaw when I realized I had let that little detail slip.

"You did." Bernadine didn't miss a beat.

"Oh nothing." I brushed it off. "And Donovan informed me that he wasn't in the market for a relationship where I saw him only at night."

I stopped. Hearing those words leave my mouth didn't sound so great. Donovan was right. The few dates that we had went on were either at his house or mine. The few sleepovers were me showing up late and needing his expertise in the computer department. And then I didn't sleep in the same room with him.

"I'm sorry, Holly. But what was that about Flora?" Bernadine showed no signs of relenting. She was determined to find out about my little disagreement with Flora.

"That's not the end of it." I followed Willow back over to the cottage steps where Bernadine had sat down on the stoop. I sat down next to her and Willow found her way into the center of Bernadine's legs. "I was so upset that I had pulled over and found myself at The Livin' End."

"No you didn't." Bernadine's eyes widened. "Were Charlie and Sean there? Because Charlie said. . ."

"Yeah. I remember all to well what she said when she dropped off those goodies for Second Cup." I sighed. "And they were there. So I went in and found them dancing to mine and Sean's song," my voice broke. "I ordered not one, but two shots of tequila."

"Holly, you have to let go of him."

"I thought I had, then I paid the bartender to interrupt the jukebox and play Elvis." I looked down at my fingers in shame. I had lowered myself to all lows.

"Not *Suspicious Minds*?" Bernadine cleared her throat when I nodded. "Oh, Holly. Did they see you?"

"They slipped out, but you know Sean. He's so street smart, he knew it was me and waited for me to leave." The more I talked, the more I was disappointed in myself for my actions. I knew better than that. "He stopped me and alluded to me that he still had something for me. He held me tight and whispered in my ear right as Donovan showed up because he felt bad for turning me away."

"No," Bernadine gasped bringing her hands to her mouth.

"Yep. I screwed up." I let out a big sigh. "Donovan said things about how beautiful he saw me and accepted me as I was. It was awful. Damn Sean," I whispered.

"What are you going to do?" Bernadine asked.

"I don't know. There is so much going on that I feel like I need to get all of this settled before I can think about dating."

"Don't worry about me." Bernadine patted my leg. "It's not looking good, kid. Tell me about Flora."

"It's nothing." I stood up and brushed myself off, trying to avoid all conversation about Flora. I was still mad that she believed Bernadine could have killed Henry. "Why doesn't it look good?"

"You know how I told you I took care of the situation, which meant the knife set." Bernadine's eyes dipped. Her lips turned down. "Officer Hart came over with a search warrant. They took apart everything in and around the house. In the row boat they found the knife set without the missing big butcher knife that someone stole and killed Henry with."

"What is Bennie saying?" I kind of knew what he had told Flora, but I wanted to hear what he had told Bernadine.

"He said it wasn't looking good. His guy couldn't find any information about the lead on Charlie but I knew if I could get this calendar, it would show something to help me." She waved the calendar in the air before she stood up and hugged me. "This might just save my ass."

“I’m surprised they didn’t arrest you.” I made a simple observation.

“I have forty-eight hours to get my affairs in order and turn myself in,” her voice choked and tears lined her eyes. “I’m in deep crap.”

“Don’t you worry about that.” I pointed to the calendar. “You take that home and try to figure out if Henry was with Charlie or Dr. Russell so we can at least give that information to them.”

“Bennie said they questioned Dr. Russell about the fight and he said it was all just professional rivalry and he had an alibi.”

“Really? I was sure he had something to do with it.”

“I’m afraid not. But someone has done a great job setting me up.” A tear trickled down her cheek. “Do you believe me when I say I didn’t do it?”

“Of course.” I reached out and rubbed down her arm.

“No one, not even Bennie believes me.” She shook her head, her red curls swung around. “He told me I should probably confess if I did it out of a crime of passion.”

"Passion?" I thought that was a funny word to use on a murder.

"I told him about Henry coming over and sweet talking me before he was killed."

"You told him about. . ." I wiggled my brows.

"Sex?" She nodded and then sighed. "Yeah. It's not looking good. I have forty-eight hours left of freedom. So I'm going to pour a large glass of wine and scour this little calendar."

"Do you want company?" I asked knowing I wasn't going to be of any use looking at her when I had to find out about Charlie.

"Nah. You have to open the shop and I'm going to go to Second Cup to meet with Sadie to see if she wants to run the shop for a few. . .," she swallowed hard, "years."

I didn't remind Bernadine that I had the Barn Dance Committee meeting this morning and I was sure Dr. Russell was going to be there, not to mention Sean since he was the contractor overseeing the build on the stages and the actual inside of the barn.

Ginger was going to meet me there so I didn't have to go by myself, plus she knew Dr. Russell pretty well. Since her family owned half of Swanee, she'd been on a lot of committees with Dr. Russell.

Willow was settled for the time being. I grabbed a quick shower and threw on my sweats, only they were way too baggy to wear. I couldn't believe it. I shut my bedroom door to look in the full-length mirror that hung on the back.

Sure enough, they didn't fit. I rotated to the left and scanned down my body, and then I did the same thing on the right. I squealed and rushed over to my closet.

"It's time." I moved the clothes hangers one-by-one down the steel rod looking for that one pair of button-up jeans I had been holding onto for years.

I pulled them out when I found them at the back of the closet and held them up in the air. Quickly I took off the baggy sweatpants and slipped on the jeans. I had to do a little sucking in to get them buttoned, but nothing too bad. The light brown sweater would cover any type of muffin top that was spilling over my jeans.

"Muffin top," I laughed and thought about Ms. Food Watchers's muffins Bernadine was selling at Second Cup.

Snort, snort. Air escaped out of Willow when she plopped back down in her dog bed.

With a giddy-up in my step with my weight loss, I grabbed my bag, phone, and keys before I darted out the door.

Food Watchers was on my way to the meeting and I had a few minutes to kill before I showed up so I popped in the Food Watchers to get a weight. I knew Bernadine wasn't probably going to go to next week's meeting and my curiosity to see what my weight loss was nagged me.

There wasn't a meeting, but the center was open during the day.

"Good morning!" The ever-so-cheerful Charlie bounced out from behind the counter. Her eyes lit up with anger. "You."

"You!" I bit back.

"What do you want?" She planted her hands on her hips. Her fancy beaded bracelets jingled. "I don't have all day. I've got to be at a meeting."

"For your design job?" I asked.

"How did you know about that?" She shifted, putting her weight on her right heel.

"I know a lot about you." I glared at her with a little bit of warning in my voice.

"Hi there," Barbie came out from the meeting room, as chipper as ever. "I have noticed your weight loss. You are looking divine." She drew her finger up and down my body.

Ahem, Charlie cleared her throat.

"You go on to your meeting. I can take care of . . .," she hesitated.

"Holly Harper." I stuck my hand out because I hadn't officially met her.

"Harper. Harper. Where have I heard that name?" Her neon pink fingernail tapped her temple. "Isn't your little boy toy. . ."

"Sean's ex." Charlie grabbed her large black fringe purse and tossed it over her shoulder along with her flowing blond hair and trotted out the door.

"I have no idea what has gotten into my sister lately, but you are going to have to excuse her." Barbie made an excuse. I could tell she had to fight an internal battle of personal restraint.

"Your sister?" I asked as shock and awe sat in my stomach.

"Yes. She looks like she'd be my sister, but it wasn't too long ago that she ate everything in her reach and looked like it too." Barbie opened a drawer at the weigh-in stand and took out a picture of a much younger version of herself and a very heavy girl next to her. "She's battled her weight all her life and I had her come work for me. I'm so proud of her. She used to be the jealous type. You know." She rotated her hand in the air. "Boys and all. Frisk. . .I know that name."

It probably shouldn't have tickled me to no end that Charlie had been fatter than I ever was, but it did. And she

knew the name Frisk. I would put money on it that Charlie had talked about Henry a time or two.

"Losing weight has given her the confidence to get a real job as an interior decorator and she's doing great. Especially here in Swanee." The pride showed on Barbie's face. "Would you like to weigh?" She put the picture on the counter and gestured to the scale.

I stepped on, looking away from the digital read out.

"Your muffins are flying off the shelf at Second Cup." I noticed there was a display of her goodies in the center with a life-sized poster of her hung next to them.

"My muffins?" she asked.

"Your low-fat pastries you are selling at Second Cup." I couldn't take my eyes off of the picture. It mesmerized me.

"I don't know what you are talking about. I only sell my stuff here." She pointed to the display of goodies. "Fresh daily. I'm so happy Charlie has taken an interest in baking with me. Since she's worked here and lost weight, she's changed. More confidence you know? Plus she has all those beading tools making that great jewelry," she gushed. "You should know! You have lost ten pounds!"

She tapped the dingy bell that was attached to the counter in celebration of my big loss, only I wasn't celebrating. The only thing I could do was smile and stand there with my mouth open after I realized Charlie had been sabotaging Bernadine this whole time.

Barbie wanted to celebrate more, but I couldn't. When she told me to wait where I was so she could get my celebratory gift for the ten-pound weight loss, I grabbed the picture and ran out of the center as fast as I could.

I jumped in the Beetle and dialed Bernadine as fast as I could.

"Hello." Bernadine answered on the first ring.

"Do not eat any more of those pastries from Barbie! She didn't make them and she knows nothing about the deal Charlie made with you to sell them."

"What are you talking about?" Bernadine asked.

"I went to Food Watchers to weigh in and Barbie was there. To make idle chit-chat I told her how her muffins were selling like hot cakes at Second Cup and she said she didn't know anything about that."

There was dead silence on the phone.

"Then she showed me a picture of a fat, F-A-T, Charlie. Fatter than me and you." I giggled. I couldn't help it. "She said Charlie has been baking with her. I think she has been baking you full fat muffins to get you to gain weight."

My head was trying to wrap around all the possibilities running through my brain.

"Bernadine," I sucked in a deep breath. "I think she has been sabotaging you to get fat because Henry must have been dating her. I bet he told her how good you were looking and she started feeding you those fat treats."

"Oh my God. All of the treats did come from her about a week after Henry moved here." Bernadine was putting together the timeline.

"And I bet they have been secretly dating for months. Then he told her he was going to get back with you." Everything I was saying made sense. "After he made love to you, I bet he told her and she killed him!"

"So all the items I have been selling at Second Cup are not low-fat?" Bernadine seemed more concerned with the goodies. "Because if I have been marketing them as low-fat, I can get in some real trouble."

"Real trouble?" I couldn't believe my ears. "You are in real trouble. Did you hear me? Noah Druck told you to get your affairs in order. That seems pretty generous considering they think you killed Henry."

"But. . .," Bernadine's voice quivered.

"No but. Charlie had to have set you up. She's a devious one." I was never so sure in my life about who had killed Henry. I couldn't wait to tell Flora that she was off. . .way off. And that Bennie needed to fire Ernie.

"All of this makes sense, but how did she get my knife?" Bernadine asked a good question. I was glad to hear her coming back to her senses.

"I don't know, but I have forty-eight hours to find out."

"Forty-four," she corrected me.

Chapter Seventeen

"I'm glad you came." Bobbi Hart waved me over when she saw me walking around the courthouse to the gazebo.

I gave her a slight wave and walked over. The lawn was filled with the business members of the community. There was a small fold-out table with a couple carafes of coffee on there with Styrofoam cups and an array of doughnuts.

"Help yourself to some coffee. It looks like you could use some." Bobbi generously noticed my bags under my eyes. "I would offer you a doughnut, but by the looks of things, you aren't eating them anymore."

"Oh." Excitement lifted my spirits. I tucked a piece of my hair behind my ear. A little embarrassed, I asked, "Can you really tell?"

"Yes. I was going to say something when you came in the office yesterday, but we got interrupted." She smiled.

It was the first time I had seen Bobbi Hart in a different light and it was nice.

"Thank you, Bobbi." I glanced down at her wrist. "That bracelet looks great on you."

"Oh I do love it." Patsy Russell said. She reached out to touch Bobbi's bracelet. "May I?"

Proudly, Bobbi stuck her wrist out for all to see.

Patsy's eyes were covered by her large-brimmed straw hat with the black polka-dot scarf neatly tied around the base of it, draping down her shoulders. Her long black hair spilled down her bare back and landed perfectly at the top of her fitted black halter dress.

"I don't think we have been properly introduced." Patsy stuck her hand out. Real diamonds dripped on her wrists along with several platinum rings across her fingers. She tipped her head to the sun. Her large blue doe eyes were mesmerizing. "I'm Patsy Russell."

"Dr. Russell's wife." I shook her hand. It was just the woman I wanted to meet.

"No." The sun hit her eyes. The deepest of blue was as bright as the diamonds on her ring. "He's Patsy Russell's husband." She winked.

There was no denying he had worked on her teeth. My eyes drifted between her perfectly white teeth and blue eyes. I couldn't stop staring. If I was right and Dr. Russell was cheating on her with Charlie, he was crazy. Patsy was hands-down the most beautiful woman in Swanee.

"Yes." I nodded and laughed. "I like that."

"My husband told me that you came in the office and mentioned to me that you suggested I come down to put my artistic ability to work." Her fancy words muddled my mind.

"Yes. Yes, I'd love to give you a free beading class." I pointed to her jewelry. "My glass beads and crystals are nothing compared to the real thing."

"Posh." She waved her hand at me. "I would love to come down there and just have some girl time. How about this afternoon?"

"Um. . ." I didn't really know what was on the calendar until I got to the shop, but I was sure I could fit her in. "Yeah, sounds great."

"Wonderful. I'll be there right after lunch." She poured herself a cup of coffee. "I'm going to grab a seat. My shins are killing me from the boot camp workout this morning."

As she walked up to the gazebo, I couldn't help but notice how toned her calves were in the high heels. Now that Donovan didn't want to see me—though I was going to change that somehow—and I didn't dare go to his self-defense class, maybe Patsy could invite me to her boot camp. After all, my calves were a little flabby where I was losing a little weight.

"There you are!" Ginger's eyes popped out of her head. She grabbed me by my hands and held me at arms length out. "I barely recognized you. I was thinking to myself, who is that hot woman Patsy Russell is talking to?"

"Thank you." I couldn't stop from smiling.

“I haven’t seen you in those jeans in a long time.” She smiled. “You look great.”

The coffee table cleared and the crowd moved toward the gazebo. Ginger and I stood back grabbing a cup of coffee.

“Did you break into Henry’s office?” she asked, scanning the area around us so no one would hear us.

“I didn’t break in. I had a key. But yes.” I took a deep breath. “Flora said that Bennie is trying to get Bernadine to confess because the evidence is so great against her.”

“She’s crazy. Bernadine couldn’t hurt a flea,” she leaned in and whispered. “But Marlene.” Her eyes shot daggers. “She’s the one to watch.”

“Come on. She is fine.” I had spent the last year trying to convince Ginger that Marlene was harmless. “Anyway, I gave the calendar to Bernadine because I couldn’t read his writing. Messy.”

“Aren’t all doctor’s handwriting scribble?” Ginger looked out at the crowd. “What did Patsy have to say?”

"She's coming in the shop today for a free beading lesson." I took a sip when someone came up to get a cup before they joined the rest of the crowd. "I'm going to question her about Dr. Russell's interior decorator who we all know is Charlie. Which reminds me. You know how Bernadine has been picking up a few pounds?"

"For goodness sakes, Holly. The woman is under a lot of stress. Stress can kill a woman's figure."

She wasn't telling me anything I didn't already know.

"I know, but I found out that the treats from Food Watchers is really Charlie's doing." My brows lifted.

"What?" The skin between Ginger's eyes wrinkled in confusion.

"Charlie is Barbie's sister. And when I went to weigh in this morning, Barbie told me that Charlie used to be fat and is jealous of all skinny people. When I told her that her pastries were flying off the shelf, she didn't know what I was talking about." I drew back and slowly nodded. Shock and awe covered Ginger's face. "Yep. She said that Charlie was an excellent baker."

"Didn't you say that Charlie wouldn't give you a sample?" Ginger asked, her eyes narrowed.

"Oh my God," I gasped. "I forgot about that. She wanted Bernadine to stay heavy while she made her move on Henry." I snapped my fingers. "And when Henry talked about Bernadine's weight loss, I bet she got jealous and started pumping Bernadine full of sugar."

"It's all making sense." Ginger looked over at the meeting as Bobbi called it to order. "I think you are going to get an ear full out of Patsy today. You need to ask her about Dr. Russell's infidelity."

"Why? Charlie probably did it alone." There really wasn't any good evidence pointing fingers at him, only the public fight.

"I had overheard his interior decorator was spying on Henry to get all the latest equipment and Henry's secret for success and telling Dr. Russell. Which means that she and Dr. Russell were working together." She took another sip of her coffee.

Slowly we walked up to the group. My mind couldn't wrap around the fact that Dr. Russell had anything to do with it.

"Did you find out from Joni if the cameras were installed?" I reminded her of her one detective job in clearing Bernadine's name.

"Yes. I mean no. Henry was still on the waiting list." She leaned over and in a low voice said, "Joni did say that he said that it was fine because he had his own way of security until we got them installed."

"What does that mean?" I asked.

She shrugged.

His own security? My mind reeled. Now would be a good time to have been speaking to Donovan. He was so good at this security computer stuff that he probably knew.

I took my phone out of my bag and looked to see if he had texted me. But he hadn't.

Can we talk? I texted him quickly and slipped the phone back in my pocket.

"Holly Harper has so graciously found time in her schedule to help out." Bobbi Hart put the spotlight on me. "Since she's great with her hands from her beading jewelry," she held her wrist in the air, "I know she's going to do a great job with the decorating committee, which meets tonight for the finishing touches. Holly, we are happy to have you. Even if it is late."

And there she went. Bobbi's specialty was digging in the gut when she didn't need to. But of course I smiled and let her have the last word.

"Bye, Holly!" Patsy called out and gave a twinkle wave. "I'll see you this afternoon."

I tilted my head back and smiled.

"I think I have been replaced." Ginger folded her arms and her jaw clenched.

I put my arm around her as we walked to our cars. "I don't know. Maybe," I joked. "Are you kidding me? No one, not even Marlene would be able to replace you." I gave her a gentle squeeze before we went our separate ways.

Do you want to meet for a coffee tonight? Donovan texted back, sending a little jolt to my heart.

The only thing I had tonight was the decorating committee meeting.

I have a committee meeting at 6 p.m. to finish the decorations for the Barn Dance but I'm sure it will be over by 7. Can you meet at 8? I texted back.

Surely it wouldn't take that long to put the finishing touches on a few decorations. Plus I wanted to make sure Donovan was going to go with me to the dance.

Dessert at 8 at Second Cup? My text dinged.

I will be there. I promise. My heart fluttered. I knew it wasn't a sure second chance but it did feel like it.

Chapter Eighteen

I flipped the sign over when I walked into The Beaded Dragonfly and pulled in the cardboard boxes full of new stock that were left by the UPS guy.

At some point I was going to have to grab Willow from home. She would be fine alone all day, but I wasn't complete without her. Plus she loved running around the shop being my little vacuum.

I cut a few of the boxes open to see what had come in.

"Yipppee!" I could hardly contain my excitement when I pulled out the plastic bag full of Celestial Crystal Beads. It was the latest trend in the fashion beaded jewelry world and they were hard to get. Every time I tried to order them, they had been on backorder.

The opaque orange with the half-coat smoky design glistened in the natural sunlight that glowed through the windows. I was definitely going to set those aside for Patsy Russell. Those gems would make her salivate and hopefully she'd open up about her husband's extra-curricular activities, by that I meant Charlie.

The bell over the door dinged, causing me to turn around.

"Noah Druck." I wasn't sure why I had said his name, but it took me aback seeing him without his Swanee police uniform on. "I was going to call you today. Or Officer Kiss."

"Because you have decided to give us the information we are seeking about Bernadine?" he asked.

"Are you on or off duty?" I wanted to know if I was on record or not. There wasn't anything I wanted to say and have it used it against me.

"I'm off duty, but I thought we could talk a bit about your Diva divorced group." He walked around the shop. He put his hand in one of the clear Swarovski crystal bins and picked up a few. He bounced his hand up and down, situating them in his palm.

Silently I squealed in fear they would bounce out of his hand and roll into the *Under*.

"Can you bring those to me?" I asked.

Problem solved. The clear beauties would go great with the new Celestial beads, which would be sure to please Patsy.

Noah walked over and put them on the counter. I scrambled to collect them as they rolled on top of the glass.

"Sorry about that." Noah's mouth spread in a frown.

"That's okay." I smiled and grabbed an empty bin from the shelf behind me, dropping them in there. I set the bin next to the Celestials. I could already see a beautiful pattern forming.

"What did you want to talk about?" he asked, referring to me telling him that I was going to call him.

"You know the unaccounted for crimp tool?" I planted my hands on the counter.

"The one that Bernadine used on her ex?"

"Funny. But no." I smiled. I knew I was about to throw him for a loop. "I found it under there." I pointed to the shelf near the bead table where Bernadine had sat the night of the murder. "I don't have a missing set of crimp tools so you can cross off the list that those came from here."

"How do I know you didn't get them in a new shipment?" He pointed to the boxes piled high near the counter.

"You can go back through all of my packaging slips." I opened the drawer where Marlene files all the packaging slips, pulled out the files, and tossed it on the counter. "I have to keep them for my accountant."

"I just might do that." The file was like candy to a kid. He couldn't resist. He opened the file and thumbed through them. "Mind if I take these with me?"

"Nope. And the credit card receipts I use for all of my purchases are in there too. You can subpoena the records, I assume."

He glanced up. He knew I was right. I could see it in his eyes. Noah Druck was never good at hiding his emotions. That was probably why it was rumored that Officer Kiss was considered the bad cop in the good cop bad cop routine they do.

"This means that whoever killed Henry Frisk, had their own crimp tool and I know Bernadine doesn't have any beading tools at her house." My brows lifted.

"I'll give you that, but," he paused. "We have the murder weapon which came from her knife set that she so happened to hide in her row boat."

He eyed me suspiciously. I stared back, knowing he was using his five senses to see if I knew something about the knife. Would he be able to use that against me and say I was a co-conspirator?

"She didn't do it." I did the cross my heart universal sign with my finger.

The evidence was against her, but someone was setting her up.

"Were her prints on the knife?" I asked. He shook his head. "You were all willy-nilly with that fingerprint powder. Were her prints anywhere in his office?"

His brows furrowed. "How do you know how much fingerprint powder we used at the scene?"

"I . . . " I swallowed hard.

"Holly Harper?" Noah leaned in a little, not once taking his eyes off of me.

"I remember how much you used in here. I can only imagine what you did there." I was quick to think on my feet.

"Well," he continued with trepidation in his voice, "who else would have access to a crimp tool, like yours, and could have used Bernadine's knife to kill Henry Frisk?"

"Charlie St. Clair." I blurted out.

"Charlie the Food Watchers specialist?" he asked with curiosity.

"Yes. She came in here with a beaded bracelet that she made at home." I shook my finger. "It wasn't just any beaded bracelet. It was flawless. Not a newbie job."

"Why on earth would a hottie, who is dating Sean," his voice escalated, " want anything to do with old Henry Frisk?"

"You tell me," I suggested. "You are the cop. All I know is Henry Frisk was seen with a blonde at The Livin' End and she was also his interior decorator for the new office."

Ding. The door opened. Patsy Russell walked in, sporting a cute denim baseball hat, denim shirt, and white denim jeans. The finishing piece was her hot pink sneakers and jewels to match.

"Hi, Officer Druck." Patsy oozed southern charm, putting Noah in her spell.

"Mrs. Russell." His face reddened. Quickly he turned back to me. "I'll look into it, Holly."

"Yeah," I warned, "you do that."

"Have a good day ladies." Noah tipped his head in the good gentlemanly fashion before he headed out the door.

I wasn't sure telling Noah what I had found out was good or bad, but the way I figured, it took some heat off of Bernadine. It would buy me time to find the real killer; while it took him time to work on the information I gave him.

Granted, I didn't know if Charlie was with Henry that night. I was relying on Agnes Pearl to get that information out of her nephew, Bradford.

"I know I'm a bit early, but I'm a little excited about using my creative side." She sat her fancy handbag on the table. "And a little girl time couldn't hurt either."

"I heard they found the knife set at—" Marlene bolted through the door with her mouth running a mile a minute. "—Bernadine's," she whispered when she saw there was a customer in the shop. "I'm sorry. I didn't know we had customers. I should really keep my mouth shut."

"I'm just one of the girls." Patsy smiled and waved off Marlene's ill manners. "Besides, I have heard all the rumors about your friend, Bernadine. But like they say, you are innocent until proven guilty."

"Finding out the murder weapon belongs to her is kind of proven if you ask me." Marlene rolled her eyes, then zeroed in on Patsy's jewels.

Patsy Russell was probably right up Marlene's alley. They both are beautiful women, who love beautiful things. Like Patsy, Marlene has only dated and married the older, wealthy men. Up until recently Dr. Russell was the only dentist around Swanee and everyone had to go to him.

"I love your lashes." Patsy got a little closer look at Marlene's face.

"They are implants." Marlene batted them.

That was all it took for the two of them to bond. I continued to do Marlene's job and empty out the boxes while she and Patsy discussed the latest trends. Marlene was drooling. The difference between her and Patsy—Patsy could afford it and Marlene could admire them from the magazines.

"That is what is so amazing about working here." Marlene walked over to the counter and picked up the Celestial beads. "These are amazing, Holly. I can't wait to design something fabulous with these."

Marlene was good because she knew if we could get Patsy Russell as a client, we would be able to make more money. Plus Marlene would have an instant friend, which Patsy was totally in the market for new friends.

Patsy's eyes grew larger under that baseball cap when Marlene dangled the strand from her fingers.

"Those are gorgeous," Patsy gasped.

She walked over and held her hand out, lightly touching the amazing orange beads.

"These would compliment the outfit I'm wearing to the Barn Dance."

Marlene placed them in Patsy's palm. Patsy was busy inspecting each one with a twinkle in her eye when Marlene turned to me and winked.

Hook, line, and sinker.

"Those are amazing. I've been waiting a few months for them." I reached over and plucked them from Patsy's hand. "I know they will sell so fast after I make a few pieces from them. Plus no one around here has any since they are so in demand in New York."

"Can I see those again?" Patsy gestured toward the Celestials.

If I sweetened the pot by adding the Swarovski crystals, I knew she wasn't going to let the Celestials go and didn't care what it was going to cost her.

"Sure." I took one of the black cloths from behind the counter to lay the beads on. The black made them pop even more. I took a handful of the clear crystals and quickly laid them up against the orange ones. “I was thinking these clear crystals would be a wonderful accent piece to the necklace and matching bracelet.”

“Oh, what about the smoky grey Swarovski?” Marlene made a great suggestion that made me a little envious that I didn’t think of it.

She walked over to the Swarovski bins and pulled some of the grey ones out, bringing them over to use and laying them on the black cloth.

Patsy’s mouth was watering.

“No one has these around here?” She couldn’t keep her fingers off of them.

“Not yet. But,” I took a calculated pause for effect, “I have a new bridal appointment today and I’m sure she’ll grab them up. These won’t last long, even at the more expensive price.”

“How much?” Patsy probed.

“The set will sell for around three hundred dollars.” I sighed before I scooped them up.

She'd had ample time to look at them.

"Even for a friend?" Worry set in her eyes.

"Hi!" The bell dinged when my new bridal appointment stepped through the door. "I'm here for my first bridal appointment." She beamed. Her eyes darted around the room.

"Hi, I'm Holly Harper." I walked around the corner of the counter with one hand out to greet the bride and the Celestials gripped in the other. "I can't wait to show. . ."

Patsy snatched the strand from my grip. "I'll take them."

"I can't wait to work with you." I smiled at the bride who was bouncing on the balls of her feet in anticipation. "Marlene, can you please go retrieve Reba's bridal box?"

"Bridal box? Is that the same thing you did for Margaret?" Reba had kept the bridal book at Margaret's wedding.

She had told me at the wedding how much she loved Margaret's jewelry and how she was going to be getting married soon. I had given her the low-down on how I

worked with my brides and gave her a card. Reba called The Beaded Dragonfly the next day to set up the appointment for today. . .months later.

Patsy was busy admiring the Celestials as I got Reba situated at the bride's table.

"Thank you, Marlene." I took the box and set it in front of Reba.

She beamed when she saw her name printed on the tag. I flipped it over so she could see the appointment tag.

"Here are the appointment times I have set up for you." I went through them one-by-one. "You need to check your calendar today and see if you need to change any of these consultations. It's important that we set all of these dates in stone in order for your custom designs to be complete by the day you walk down that aisle."

"I will make them work." Reba ran her hands along her box. "I've been waiting months for this day. I can't wait to see what you can design for my vintage lace gown I'm using. It was my grandmother's." There was pride in her voice.

“Wonderful.” I clasped my hands together and pinched my lips tight.

Poor girl. There was a time I was her. Now I was far from how she felt and wanted to tell her to run. Run far, far away.

“I want you to take a look at these design magazines. List at least six things you like. Not the actual full design, but if you like the way one clasp is or how the necklace lays on the neck.” I pushed a couple of the jewelry magazines closer to her. “I’m going to get my other client started and be back in a few minutes.”

Eagerly, Reba didn’t waste time. She opened the first magazine with a smile curling up one corner of her mouth.

Marlene had brought out the bridal champagne and gave Patsy a glass too. The two of them were getting along swimmingly. Marlene had already sat Patsy at a table and gotten a bead board from the back of the shop and was showing Patsy all the tools she was going to need to create her masterpiece.

Patsy looked lost and for a second I thought she was going to talk Marlene into making the piece, but I had to keep her here. I needed information about Dr. Russell and his relationship between Charlie and Henry Frisk.

"I can help if you need me." I walked up behind them and looked at the bead board. I arranged a few beads sitting there to give Patsy a pattern to work with. "I think you need some Bali beads to give it the dark look you are aiming for."

The Bali beads were the more ornamental silver beads. They were also very expensive, but it would compliment her piece to exactly the standards she was used to.

"These are beautiful too." The glint in her eye showed me she didn't care what I put on there and she'd fall in love with it.

Reba had a question and Marlene rushed over to help her while I started to work on Patsy.

"Your husband did a great job on my teeth last week." I looked over her expression with a critical eye to see if she had any reaction.

"He is a great dentist." She wrinkled her nose and her shoulders lifted as if an invisible wire connected them. "He will take wonderful care of you."

"You know," I leaned in and whispered so she would think it was just between girl friends, "I had gone to Henry Frisk and he was terrible."

"We don't have to worry about him anymore." She continued to move the beads around in the ugliest design I had ever seen. "I am wearing a little orange plaid shirt and the most fabulous hat to top it off."

"Plus Henry was more concerned about the interior decorating of the office than his clients." I shook my head and rearranged the beads again. "It is decorated nicely. I wonder who did it?"

"Buskin's Designs is doing Kevin's new office." She rolled a crystal between her pink tinted fingernails, and with her self-assured confidence she said, "They are okay. But I'd get a different designer if I were you."

"I don't know who is working with you on your husband's office, but I know that Charlie," I snapped my fingers together as though I had forgotten her last night.

"Charlie St. Clair from Buskins?"

"Yes!" I clapped my hands together. "Bernadine said that she not only did Henry's office, but she was trying to get her claws into him."

Patsy's eyes flew open. Her mouth dropped. Something flickered in her eyes.

"And he and Bernadine were going to get back together too." I nodded my head. "Mmm, hmm." I shook my head.

"That's terrible what happened to him." Patsy put her hand to her chest. The big diamond on her left hand was bigger than any gem I had in The Beaded Dragonfly. "Kevin and I couldn't believe it when we heard. You know," she tugged me closer to her, "since we are girl-friends," she paused as if she was waiting to confirm.

My head nodded like it was on a spring.

"Kevin and Henry had a fight at one of the barn dance meetings over Henry stealing Kevin's clients."

My eyes widened encouraging her to continue.

"The police even came to our house to ask us about it." She sucked in a deep breath. "They wanted to know if my Kevin had anything to do with Henry's murder."

"The nerve." I quipped. "Kevin wouldn't hurt a fly. Would he?"

"Never. Gentle, gentle man." Her eyes darted around the shop and slid back to me. "In fact, that little Charlie tramp even hit on my Kevin."

"No." I took a quick breath as if I was taken by surprise. Which I wasn't in the least bit.

She shrugged, a delicate movement that spoke volumes.

"I'm so sorry. We Divas wouldn't put up with that." My brows lifted. "Did you catch them?"

"No. Carol told me." Patsy looked away. There were tears in her eyes. "When I asked Kevin about it, he said that I was all he needed and he gave me this." She shifted the side of her head. The diamond-studded earrings were just as big as the diamond on her finger.

"Gorgeous." I smiled. "He loves you so much."

Snake. Patsy smiled back and continued to arrange the beads. Did she really believe he wasn't sleeping with Charlie?

"If it weren't for all the evidence against Bernadine Frisk, Kevin and I believed that Charlie might have killed him."

"Really?" I didn't give her eye contact. I kept my fingers busy as though I was really trying to get her a design she was going to love. "Why would you say that?"

"Kevin told me that he went to Henry's office before Henry opened to wish him luck." I leaned in closer to hear her. "He said that he saw her sitting on Henry's lap in his office chair with her dress unzipped to her waist while Henry was kissing her neck."

"What did Henry say to Kev. . .Dr. Russell?" I asked, a little more curious.

"He didn't see Kevin. Kevin said he slipped out unseen." She licked her pink lips. "Do you think Bernadine found out and killed him?"

"I don't know. I'm just trying to support her through it."

I unrolled a long piece of wire for Patsy. It was probably a good time to take a break from all the Henry talk.

"This is the wire you are going to string your beads on." I showed her. "I'm going to have you string a few beads, lay it across your wrist so you can see if you like the design I have here."

She leaned over the board. There was satisfaction on her face.

"This is a crimp bead." I held the tiny silver cylinder in the palm of my hand. I pointed to the crimp tool. Every time I saw one, I thought of Bernadine. "This is a crimp tool. First you use the second indent to smash the crimp bead like this." I showed her how I flattened the bead. "Then you have to make a little fold so the clasp will stay in place." I took the tool and put the flattened crimp bead in the opposite direction, making it fold in half.

"Oh!" Patsy was excited. "I think I can do that."

She picked up a loose piece of wire and strung a crimp bead on it. She used the crimp tool and with a little assistance, she made it perfectly like I taught her.

"I want you to practice crimping so you can learn how to put on a clasp." I left a few of the crimp beads and stray wire on her board before I went to check on Reba, who was on her third round of champagne.

"How is it going?" I asked and picked up the bottle holding it out for Marlene to take.

"I'm just so confused." Reba slurred. "I thought I was going to come in here and nail exactly what I wanted." She held up the magazine. "There are so many choices." She giggled.

"Okay." I looked at the clock and took a deep breath. The Divas were coming soon and I wanted Reba and Patsy gone. "What color are you going to use for your bridesmaids? We can start there."

"I'm thinking. . ." She patted her temple with fingertip and slowly pointed it at Patsy and Marlene. "That she's a bitch." Reba's head lowered and hit the table.

"Shit." I murmured looking at the passed out Reba. "Marlene?" I called her over.

"What the hell?" Marlene let out a raspy chuckle.

"You kept filling up her drink." My blood pressure rose. I had never had a drunk bride before. "Can you sit here with Reba and act like you are consoling her so I can get Patsy out of here before the Diva meeting?"

"How is it going?" I looked over Patsy's shoulder.

"I'm getting a little better." She held a couple of the crimped wire strands in the air. Some were good, but most were bad.

"You are." I assured her. "I think this is enough for today. What about you come back tomorrow for your second lesson?"

"Oh." There was a grunt of disappointment from her. "I thought we could grab lunch."

"I wish." I rolled my eyes. "I have a full list of clients today. But another time for sure."

"Okay. Sounds great." She stood up and grabbed her clutch. "Don't let anyone have my beads."

"Don't you worry about that." I was a little disappointed that I didn't get any real information from her about Henry and Dr. Russell's fight. "I did want to tell you that you need to make sure that Carol gives out the toothbrush and mini-toothpaste at the end of each visit to Dr. Russell."

"You didn't get one?" she asked.

"No. And I needed a new toothbrush too." That was the only time I got new toothbrushes. Now I had to go buy one.

"Ugh." Patsy gave a polite laugh. "If you only knew how many times we have told her to give out the packets."

I walked her to the door.

"In fact, I think I have some of the new packs in the back of my car." She gestured me to follow her.

"I'll be right back." I told Marlene and walked out of the shop.

Patsy's fancy two-door Mercedes coupe was parked right in front of the shop. Her license plate read DR WIFE.

"I love your license." I snickered.

"If you only knew how much I had to keep up my appearance. Being a doctor's wife isn't easy." She pushed a button on her keyfob and the trunk popped open. She looked me up and down. "You have no idea how much I'd like to dress down like you."

I wasn't sure if it was a compliment or not, but I let it roll off of me. The cutest green tote bags filled the back of her car. She grabbed one and handed it to me.

Dr. Russell's logo was printed on the front. There was a travel coffee mug, magnet, toothbrush, floss, toothpaste, and mouthwash inside.

"Wow. This is like Christmas." I was set.

"We have a new Keurig coffee machine that is going to be in the lobby for clients." She smiled. "I'm thrilled

Kevin finally listened to me about remodeling his office. He can be an old fogey sometimes."

"Thank you so much. I'm glad I waited." I held the bag in the air and waved her off.

Chapter Nineteen

"What are we going to do with her?" I pointed to the passed-out Reba. "Now I'm going to have to give her jewelry to her for free."

"No you won't." Marlene had that *I know what to do* look in her eye. "We can come up with her design and tell her that she picked it out before she took a nap. Kind of like Jedi mind tricks."

"You have come up with some off beat stuff, but this one takes the cake." I wasn't buying into any Jedi crap. I never saw Star Wars, much less knew anything like what Marlene was talking about.

"Think about it," Marlene pleaded, rushing around to every bin, picking out all sorts of crazy color combinations. "We can convince her that she was under so much stress that she just is plumb exhausted."

"Hmm..." The idea was crazy, but it just might work. "We could do a simple silver and clear design mostly made up of some of the antiqued bone beads." They would match Reba's vintage dress with the look of lace provided on the beads. Plus there was a focal oval design with a flower inset on it that would match perfectly.

As if on cue, Marlene grabbed a few of the beads and quickly got to work on a basic, but simply beautiful pair of earrings that any bride would want to wear.

While Marlene worked, I put Dr. Russell's client pack behind the counter and got out the Diva's bead boards. If they were going to be here, they might as well keep their hands busy while their mouths were talking. We were all working on a friendship bracelet made up of a few Bali rondelles and round sterling silver six millimeters between. I had gotten each of us a "D" charm and our initials put on the back. We are the original Divas and I wanted to make sure we all had a fun way to show it.

One-by-one, they trickled in. Bernadine was the first, packing all the goodies that Charlie had sent to Second Cup.

"What are you doing? Trying to sabotage us all?" I asked, giving her a frown as Ginger walked in behind her.

"I can't believe it. I trusted that girl." Bernadine jabbed her fist in the air. "Was she that insecure to think Henry really wanted me over her?"

Suddenly Bernadine started to cry.

Ginger rushed over to her and put her arms around her as more Divas filed in.

"Do you really think he wasn't sincere the night he died?" Ginger asked knowing how much Bernadine was still in love with Henry Frisk even though he was an ass.

"He talked a good talk, but he always did." Bernadine took a tissue from Agnes Pearl.

"They all do, honey." Agnes tsked and adjusted her turban of choice for the meeting. A hot pink number with a large black feather jutting out the back.

"Oh," I remembered. "I found a feather at Henry's office."

"A feather?" Flora's eye narrowed. "You didn't say anything about a feather."

"What does that have to do with Henry?" Cheri didn't care about the calories in the muffin she was stuffing in her face.

"I don't know." I picked up one of the pretzel sticks dipped in chocolate that Charlie had given Bernadine and took a bite. "It just seemed really out of place. There weren't any feather things in his office. Not even a pillow where a feather could float out of."

The pretzels were so good, I went back for seconds.

"It would seem odd since Henry hated birds." Bernadine gave a little bit of trivia. "Where would it have come from?"

Agnes Pearl straightened up. "The outside. There are birds all around this city." She laughed. "One could've floated right through the door. Just like on that movie Forrest Gump. There was a feather floating all around him." She glared. "I never understood that part in the movie."

"Anyway, I found it weird." I shrugged. "Did you figure out anything from the calendar?"

"No." Sadness crossed her face. "It's like code or something."

"Agnes," I got her attention.

She was hunched over the bead board trying to string a few beads on her friendship bracelet.

"Did you talk to Bradford?" I was hoping she had quizzed her nephew about seeing Henry and the blonde.

"Yep. Sure enough it was Charlie." The lines on her forehead deepened. "He said he had seen them a few times. She was at Henry's office when Bradford got his teeth cleaned and again when he got his crown put on. Once they were in a compromising position." She wiggled her brows.

"That is what Patsy Russell told me too." I told them her story about Dr. Russell going to see Henry and how Charlie was all up in Henry's lap. The story only made Bernadine cry more, which made her realize that Henry Frisk only *wanted* her to believe that he wanted her back because he loved her, *not* because he didn't want to pay her anymore.

"What about you, Cheri? Did you get an appointment with Dr. Russell?" I asked, following up on her task.

"Yes. Carol told me that they were shutting down the office for a couple weeks for remodel." She let out a heavy sigh. "I'm sorry I couldn't get in front of him any sooner."

"No problem." Bernadine gave a small smile of gratitude. "At least you tried."

"Ginger." I looked over at my best friend. "Any more from Joni?"

"Nope. Still the fact remains, Henry's office was on the waiting list for the security system," she said.

"The bill collector for Buskin's called me. They said I had to pay Henry's bill or they were going to sue me." Bernadine interrupted our round table discussion. She could tell none of us were getting any closer to solving who killed her ex. "Could this week get any worse?"

Before she could shut her mouth, the bell over the door dinged. Office Kiss walked in and headed straight to Bernadine.

"Ms. Frisk." Officer Kiss stood with her legs hip-width apart. She reached behind her and pulled the cuffs off her utility belt. "I'm placing you under the arrest for the murder of Henry Frisk. You have the right. . ."

Helplessly, the Divas stood there with our mouths open. It didn't even phase me that Agnes had held her unfinished bracelet in the air and all the beads had tumbled into the *Under.*

Bernadine didn't resist. She stood up and took it like a true lady. Her chin cocked in the air, but there was fire in her eyes.

"I'll call Bennie." Flora wasted no time getting her phone and punching the keyboard for Bennie's number. When he answered, she talked swift and fast. "He's on his way to the station. Don't say a word. He will meet you there."

Neither Officer Kiss nor Bernadine said a word as Officer Kiss directed Bernadine out to her squad car and stuck Bernadine in the back. Flora didn't waste any time getting to her car and peeling off down the road. No doubt

in my mind, I knew she was going to beat Bernadine and Bennie to the station.

This was a day the Divas would not forget. Seeing one of our own in the rear window of a cop car was far from our intentions of the group.

“Now what?” Agnes Pearl wrung her wrinkled hands together.

“We wait,” I said.

“Wait?” Cheri didn’t seem to like my idea.

“Wait until we hear from Flora. Until we hear all the charges.” In reality, I wasn’t sure what we were supposed to do. “Until then, I’m going to run my shop and continue to hunt for clues to get this thing straightened out.”

“Don’t forget about the decorating meeting tonight at the barn.” Ginger reminded me.

I grabbed the floss out of Dr. Russell’s bag and pulled a long piece out, cutting it on the silver tab. Carefully I ran the floss in my back teeth to get the pretzel bits from between them.

"I'll be there." I wasn't sure why I was going to go there, but I would keep the commitment. "What are we going to do about Charlie?"

I looked at each of them.

"What are you going to do about her?" Agnes Pearl lowered her glasses down on the edge of her nose. Her beady eyes peered over them.

All of our heads turned toward Reba who was waking up.

"Reba!" I rushed over forgetting all about her. "I love these. Great choice."

Marlene rushed over as I continued with our little plotted plan to throw off tipsy Reba who definitely couldn't control her alcohol and shoved the pieces she had made in Reba's face.

Reba was a little disoriented, but smiled when she saw "her" ideas come to life.

"I did pick out some nice beads, didn't I?" She wanted confirmation.

"Beautiful." Cheri confirmed and walked over taking a closer look at the earrings that did turn out very nice. "You are going to look stunning."

"Thank you." Reba still had a confused look on her face, but she bucked up and did her best to cover it up.

"We have our next appointment scheduled." I gestured to help her up. Marlene put the earrings in Reba's bride box and whisked it off to the back. "I'll see you then."

Still dazed, Reba smiled and nodded, quietly walking out of The Beaded Dragonfly. I locked the door behind her and flipped the sign.

"I think we all need to go around town and dig a little more. Think," I encouraged them. "Ask people. People in Swanee love to gossip. We have to help Bernadine."

I glanced at the phone hanging on the wall hoping it would ring and that Flora would be on the other line. It didn't. We sat in silence for a few minutes.

Finally, Agnes Pearl stood up and broke the tension.

"Well, I don't think Bernadine did it. And it's just like an ex-ass to get the last laugh." She adjusted her turban and waddled out of the shop.

"We'll see who gets the last laugh," I muttered under my breath when all the Divas had left. "Charlie thinks she's fooled us all, even her sister. She better think again."

Chapter Twenty

I ran home to check on Willow to make sure she was okay and took her for a quick walk around the lake. The pretzels and chocolate were loaded with fat and it was the last thing I needed to eat. I had spent a good part of the afternoon trying to get the damn things out of my teeth with no luck. Dr. Russell's floss was the kind that didn't have wax. And I liked the wax. Slipped in and out easy. No fuss. No blood.

There hadn't been any time to do laundry so I put the jeans back on that I had walked in with Bernadine and had worn the day before. They were already dirty and if I was going to be decorating a barn, there was no need to put on good clothes.

On the way to the meeting, I reached over to my console of my Beetle and got out the floss Bernadine had given me from Henry's new office.

"Ha! Wax." I read the label and happily tore off a large piece.

Just like I knew it would, the floss glided between my teeth, grabbing all those pretzels pieces Dr. Russell's floss couldn't. I made a mental note to tell Patsy at our bead meeting tomorrow about how she needed to get wax floss instead of the non-wax. I put the floss in my jean pocket just in case I needed it later.

The gazebo was in the open courtyard right behind the courthouse. The twinkle lights were already positioned around the top of the century-old wooden structure, through the lattice, and around the pillars. The performance stage will feature Swanee's finest talents, including cloggers and local musical acts. The folding chairs and picnic tables dotted the courthouse lawn.

The old barn was directly behind the gazebo. It looked like a few men were in there building the dance floor.

"Holly!" Ginger waved her arms in the air.

She was in the front row. Her hair was pulled up into a loose ponytail. She wore a long flowing dress and jeweled sandals to match. She looked like she was still on the vacation she just got home from.

"I didn't mean to sit right up front." I sat next to her in one of the empty seats. "No one wants to sit up front." I hung my bag on the back of the fold up chair. "Shit," I whispered when I saw Sean and Charlie walking down the middle aisle.

I slumped down in my chair and ran my fingers through my hair.

"Holly." Sean acknowledged me when he took the seat next to me and Charlie took the seat next to him.

"Sean." I planted a fake grin on my face. Briefly, I glanced over at Charlie. Killer. "Charlie."

One of the committee chairmen brought the meeting to order before Charlie could even speak which was fine with me.

I had no idea what the chairman and Bobbi were talking about and really didn't care since I was there for one reason only. I looked around to see if I could find Dr. Russell and I continued to keep my eye on Charlie.

"Are you okay?" Ginger tapped my leg. The crickets chirped in the background helping disguise our whispers.

"I'm fine." I swallowed hard and shook the notion that Dr. Russell and Charlie had somehow made some elaborate scheme to kill Henry.

Out of the corner of my eye, I saw a man that looked a lot like Dr. Russell stand up and walk toward the back. Out of the other corner of my eye, Charlie put her long fingers on Sean's thigh and whispered something in his ear before she got up and walked toward the back.

I waited a second, trying to gather my thoughts before I whispered in Ginger's ear, "I need to pee."

"Now?" she asked.

I didn't bother answering in fear I would miss out on where Charlie and Dr. Russell had gone. All the seats were filled and there was standing room only on the courtyard ground. I walked on my tiptoes to see if I could see over everyone's head, but since I was vertically challenged—short—I picked up the pace. When I got to the back of the

group, I looked left and right but didn't see Charlie or Dr. Russell.

The large glass courthouse door that was up the steps in front of me, swayed a little, as if someone had gone in. I looked at my watch. It was well after seven and I knew they closed at five.

"Not if you have a key because you are redecorating the courthouse." I whispered. A little tickled hit erupted in my gut when I realized that Charlie was probably the designer and it would be a perfect place for her and Dr. Russell to have a little rendezvous.

One-by-one I took the marble courthouse steps up to the large glass door. I inhaled deeply and gripped the brass handle. Slowly I glanced behind me to see if anyone was looking. When I saw that the coast was clear, I opened the door and slid in.

The century-old courthouse was creepy during the day, downright terrifying at night. The red dot on the fire alarms and sprinkle system was the only light, which was no bigger than an ant on the wall.

"What did you say?" A voice echoed down the hallway.

Lightly, I walked down the hall, following the murmurs. I stopped shy of the door where the light was coming from. With my backside and palms pressed up against the wall, I slid my way along until I reached the crack of the slightly open door.

Charlie and Dr. Russell were about an inch apart. Charlie continually wiped her eyes as though she had been crying.

"I didn't say anything," Charlie said. "There wasn't anything to say."

"Did you say anything about me wanting you to spy on him?" Dr. Russell grabbed her by the arms and jerked her to look up at him.

"No. They are assuming I smacked him at the bar because they believe he told me he was getting back with that fat wife of his." She jerked away and stepped back. "When I really smacked him for grabbing my ass."

"You keep doing what you are doing. Including the baked good for Barbie and keep your mouth shut," Dr. Russell warned.

A deep-set fear made me rush back down the hall and into the shadows of the courthouse when I realized they were coming out of the room.

"I will meet you at the office tomorrow at lunch to discuss the plans." Dr. Russell walked behind Charlie giving him instructions. "The Barn Dance is in a couple of days and hopefully Bernadine will be in jail and this whole mess will be over. No one ever has to know."

"How do I look?" Charlie turned around and tousled her hair, making me all sorts of jealous. I never looked that good after I cried. "I can't let Sean see me like this."

"You keep Sean oblivious to what is going on. Hear me?" Dr. Russell swept a strand of Charlie's hair behind her shoulder before he tucked his hand behind her neck. Bringing her closer to him, his lips covered hers in the most passionate kiss I had ever seen. Certainly one I had ever seen a doctor give to his interior decorator.

"Shit. Shit. Shit." My mind was reeling after they let themselves leave one before the other, giving them enough space so members of the committee wouldn't notice them together. I took my cell out of my pocket. I had to get ahold of anyone. Someone. "Charlie and Dr. Russell killed Henry."

I held the phone in the air trying to get some reception.

"You knew the whole time." Sean came out of the shadow and into the dimly lit hallway. "You knew she was playing me for some type of fool and laughing your ass off."

"No. No I had no idea." I took my hands out of the air. "But I think she and Dr. Russell killed Henry."

"Why do you think that?" he asked.

"Because she was the interior decorator for Henry. She had access to his office. She went on a date with Henry before she cherry-picked you and she just kissed Dr. Russell." I put my phone back in my pocket.

If I had to get all of this off my chest and Sean was the only one there to be a sounding board. . .so be it.

Damn, did he look good. And his natural scent that drove me crazy when we were younger and got me into bed, was even more aromatic tonight.

"That makes her a killer?" He laughed and ran his hands through his loose locks. "She isn't a killer."

"Dr. Russell didn't want the competition from Henry. I know Henry was taking all his clients from him and Dr. Russell would stop at nothing to get rid of Henry."

"He didn't kill Henry, Holly." Sean looked down at his feet. "Bernadine did."

"She did not," I defended her.

"They made an arrest as soon as she left your shop tonight." Sean's eye stared at me intently as if he was trying to see what I was going to do.

There was no time to waste. I rushed to the door and tugged on the handle. I had to get to Bernadine as fast as I could. I had to give Noah Druck the information about Dr. Russell and Charlie's affair.

"Why won't it open?" I tugged harder.

"Bernadine had the most to lose." Sean continued to talk as I continued to tug. That was one quality of his that didn't fit into our relationship. He loved to ignore me. "There was a five million dollar insurance policy on his life in Bernadine's name. If he died before the end of the alimony payments, she was to be awarded five million dollars."

"Five what?" I shook my head in disbelief. "Did you and Charlie knock back a few before the meeting?"

I pulled on the handle more.

"Open!" I screamed and banged on the glass. I put my hands over my eyes and shielded them to look out at the Barn Dance meeting, but it looked like they had dissipated and everyone had gone into the barn, way across the lawn. "Shit. We are locked in here and no one can hear us."

I planted my back up against the glass door and slid down with my hands in my face.

"Did you hear me?" Sean babbled on while I tried to think of ways to get out of here. . .away from him.

"Phone! Donovan!"

Donovan. . .my stomach churned. I had completely missed our eight o'clock Second Cup dessert date because I was stuck in here with Sean. I held the phone in the air and swirled it around when I saw that I still didn't have any bars. I felt sick. I was already walking a thin line with our rocky relationship, no thanks to me.

"Donovan. Weee!" Sean waved his hands in the air and began to clap. "Yippee! Donovan can come save us. Poor us, helpless us. *Right,"* he mocked me. "And you won't be able to use your phone in here. All the equipment blocks the cell tower signals."

"He's going to be so mad at me."

"I hope you tell him you were with me." Sean grinned and winked. "It will send macho man right over the edge."

"Shut up," I snapped. "What did you say about five million dollars?"

“Sweet Bernadine had it out for Henry.” Sean popped a squat next to me after he took a tug on the door handle. “She didn’t like the fact that he was taking her back to court to stop the alimony. I guess she left out the little bit of information about the five million dollar life insurance policy she made him take out to ensure she got her full installment of the alimony payments even after death.”

“Wait,” I interjected. “Are you telling me that there was a life insurance policy worth five million dollars payable to Bernadine?”

“Yes. If Henry was alive and finished out the alimony payments, the life insurance policy was voided. If Henry died before the alimony payments were complete per the divorce decree, then Bernadine was the beneficiary of the five million dollar policy.” He tapped his temple and leaned over. He whispered, his breath hot against my cheek, “One smart divorcée.”

“And that proves she killed him?” I asked, knowing it was a great reason to kill someone.

"Come on, Holly." His face contorted. "Five. Million. Dollars."

"Too bad you weren't worth that much and I didn't have that policy or you would've been dead a long time ago." I sat shocked.

Why didn't Bernadine tell me about the policy?

"That can't be true." I turned to Sean, not looking into his green eyes. "Bernadine didn't have the crimp tool. It was in the *Under*."

"What?" Sean had a perplexed look on his face.

Quickly I gave him the run down on the crimp tool and how I knew Charlie had been making bracelets at home.

"Charlie may be a lot of things. And I mean that. . ." His lips turned up like he had a dirty little secret about her, but knew not to tell me. "But she is not a killer. Killer body maybe."

"Shut up!" I pushed him over and he laughed the whole time.

"Holly, she isn't a woman like you." He sat back up. His jaw tensed. His eyes locked with mine for a moment too long.

My heart fluttered. I took a deep gulp as his upper body leaned in a little too close.

"I have to get out of here." I stood up and dusted off my backside. "There is no way she killed Henry. Money or not."

Something didn't add up and I was going to figure it out.

"They aren't going to hear you." Sean's harsh laughter echoed throughout the halls of the courthouse as he got a kick out of me pounding on the glass.

"What time is?"

"Why? We aren't going anywhere anytime soon."

"What time is it?" I screamed and grabbed my phone. "Nine o'clock. Shit! Shit!"

I could picture Donovan over at Second Cup waiting on me. Another chance and I blew it.

"Were you and muscle man supposed to go out tonight?" Amusement danced around Sean's face and his dimples deepened when he saw the look on my face and he was right. The look I always hated. "I'm right, aren't I?"

"Shut up." I slid back down the glass door, giving up on all hopes. There was no way I was going to be able to explain to Donovan what had happened. Twice in two days with Sean. It was over. "You can't just leave well enough alone. Why? Why Sean? You don't want me. You just want to say that I fell for you all over again, just so you can break my heart."

About that time, I heard footsteps walking up the marble courthouse steps outside.

Ginger's face planted up against the glass door looking into the darkness of the courthouse.

"Ginger!" I jumped to my feet and banged on the door. "We are in here!"

"Okay! Hold on. I will get someone." She rushed off.

"Thank God I don't have to be in here with you any longer." I threw my arms down to my side. "Ouch!" I yelled out when something poked me.

I put my hands in my pocket and pulled out the piece of metal Willow had found under the rock at Bernadine's house and the feather from Henry's office. I put them back in my pocket when I saw Ginger and Patsy walking up.

They got the door open with a key.

"Patsy was talking to the Mayor about his remodel and he gave us the keys to let you out." Ginger and Patsy looked at us suspiciously. "What were you two doing in there?"

"I came in to go to the bathroom and he followed me." I shrugged and walked out before the glass door closed again on me. "He's asking me out. Right Sean?"

I didn't wait for him to answer. I grabbed Ginger on one side of me and Patsy on the other as we made our way to the barn.

Chapter Twenty One

"How long were you in there?" Patsy blue eyes practically leapt out of their sockets with concern. "I would have a nervous breakdown if I was in that creepy place in the dark."

She handed the keys off to the Swanee mayor as we passed him. He smiled and she gave him a sweet smile and quick thank you.

"And with Sean." Ginger wasn't going to let that part go. "Was he really hitting on you? What about Charlie?"

"Charlie?" Patsy's hat flew when she lifted her head. "Charlie St. Clair?"

"Long, long, long story." I bent down and picked up the Burberry-inspired hat.

The straw fedora had the infamous Burberry plaid fabric around the base of it, giving it the touch of class we all knew Patsy encouraged. I handed it back to her.

"Cool hat," I said with a bit of jealousy in my gut.

Patsy Russell was stylish, beautiful and much nicer than Charlie. Kevin Russell would be crazy to cheat on her, which made me think I was way off base with him being part of Henry's murder, though Charlie was still number one suspect in my book.

"I love this one. I've had it so long that I don't even mind the wear and tear." Patsy laughed and brushed off the brim before she stuck it back on her head. "I'm missing some bling and feathers, but I think I like it better without them."

"Still cute." Ginger gestured to the table where all the strings of lights still needed to be strung. "Let's go help out over there."

I looked around. Sean and Charlie were in a heated conversation at the front of the stage, away from the lights. That was where I needed to be. . .away from him.

"I'm going to work on the table decorations." Patsy waved bye and headed over to the adorable table lanterns where they were putting cute bling and candles in them.

That was definitely her cup of tea. Bling looked good on and around her.

“Spill it.” Ginger walked over and picked up the balled-up, mangled set of lights that was going to keep us busy for a while.

“More than ever I believe that Charlie had something to do with Henry.” I could feel it in my gut. I wasn’t sure what it was, but it was something. “When Patsy came to the shop, she confirmed that Henry and Charlie were having an affair. But. . .” I bit the edges of my lip. I looked over at Charlie. My eyes clouded with anger as she and Sean seemed to be making up. “Sean told me that Bernadine stood to gain millions of dollars upon the death of Henry Frisk to pay out the rest of the alimony. And if Henry changed the alimony, the insurance policy would be deleted too.”

“So that was the evidence they had to arrest her?” Ginger’s eyes grew bigger.

“Yeah.” I didn’t understand why Bernadine hadn’t told any of us about it.

"That's a big deal." Ginger held up the ball of lights, sighed, and put them back down. "It gives her motive much larger than killing for alimony. Especially if it's millions."

"That's what I thought too. But why didn't she ever mention it?" I asked. "I walk with her every day and she never mentioned it. Ever."

"Some people don't like to talk about money." Ginger handed me the ball of lights. "Do you think you can figure this out?"

"Can I talk to you?" Charlie walked up behind us unannounced.

"I'll go get us a drink." Ginger looked between me and Charlie before she bolted off.

The noise of the decorating committee seemed to lower to a hush whisper. I didn't want to look to see if they were watching what was going on between Charlie and me so I kept playing it cool.

"Sure." I shrugged and sat down on the barn floor. I winced in pain from a jab in my pocket. "I have to keep working on these lights if we are ever going to get them up before tomorrow night."

"I hear you are asking all sorts of questions about my relationships with Dr. Russell and Henry Frisk." Charlie didn't have as much of a problem popping a squat on the barn floor as I did.

I put my hand in my pocket and pulled out the metal piece from the dental floss, Henry's dental floss, and Dr. Russell's dental floss along with the infamous feather.

"I'm not saying I wasn't in the beginning stages of a relationship with Henry when he was killed, but he made it clear that he wanted to try to make it work with his ex-wife." Her hooded eyes swept past my shoulder.

I put the floss down on the ground and turned to see what she was looking at. Sean was talking with Patsy and I bet it made Charlie jealous. Sean and Patsy looked over at us staring at them. Patsy's face hardened when she saw Charlie.

"Henry told you that the night of his death at The Livin' End and you killed him for it." I fanned the feather in the air. "You killed Henry Frisk."

"I did not kill Henry," she whispered through gritted teeth. "Bernadine did. She found out about the affair and she killed him."

"So why were you fattening her up?" I asked.

"How did you know about that?" Tears clouded those big beautiful eyes of hers and it made me happy that she was an ugly crier.

"It doesn't take a rocket scientist to realize you refused to give me a piece, but fed Bernadine like I feed my pig. Bernadine was doing everything right to lose weight. But putting two and two together was part of it. The icing on the puzzle was when your sister, Barbie, told me all about poor pitiful young Charlie who would sabotage anyone to get what she wanted." I jabbed the feather in her face. "You wanted Henry Frisk. Let me tell you something." My face was inches from hers. "You don't need to kill me off to get your paws on my ex-ass. You can have him."

I stood up and dusted myself off.

"I'm going to find Sean." Charlie glared at me. She held her hand out. "Do you want me to give Patsy her feather back?"

"What?" My nose curled in disgust.

"The feather." She held out her hand. "It goes in the side of the Burberry Fedora. Pasty's missing hers." She looked around. "I'm sure no one else here has the same hat, though I want one. But I couldn't afford one."

"Are you sure?" I asked eagerly.

"Yes. I know my fashion," she said matter-of-factly.

"Where did they go?" The clues started adding up in my head. "I have got to find Sean."

"I thought you said that. . ." There was intensity in her lowered voice.

"Never mind what I said!" I took off in a mad dash. "I've got to find him!"

I bolted out the door with the feather in my grip. I had to find Sean. I didn't know where they went. All I knew was that he was in the hands of a cold-blooded killer.

"Hey Holly!" Reba darted to the side when I almost ran smack dab into her.

"Hey! I. . .I have to go," I said in a haste.

"I wanted to thank you for having me there today. I'm so looking forward to working with you." She grabbed my arm. "I love the design. But I have to confess that I was a little taken aback to see Patsy Russell in your shop."

"Patsy?" I stopped fighting her to get away.

"Yeah, Patsy Russell has the best beaded jewelry collection and she wasn't shy pointing out to Margaret McGee and her mom the flaws in all of the jewelry you made for Margaret." Reba's eyes smoldered with fire as she continued to talk. "I told Margaret not to listen to her. She even took Margaret's bride box home with her and tried to fix what she said was messed up, but Margaret's mom got wind about what Patsy was doing and marched

over to the Russell mansion demanding Patsy give back the box."

"Wait." I shook my head because it was having a hard time wrapping around what Reba was telling me. "You are telling me that Patsy had access to Margaret's bride box?"

Everything started to add up in my head like a cash register.

"Yep. And when I saw her today, I had to chug down that champagne to even deal with the fact she was there." Her brows rose. "In fact, Patsy lost her only friend that day. Mrs. McGee."

"Thanks, Reba!" I jumped up on my toes. "You didn't happen to see Patsy just now did you?"

"Yeah." Reba pointed toward town in the direction of the police station and Henry Frisk's office. "She jumped in an old truck with some hot guy. Probably another man that would stand in the way of her money like Dr. Frisk."

"Dr. Frisk?" I asked. My stomach knotted in fear.

"Mrs. McGee said that Patsy wouldn't stand for any competition for her hubby and dare risk losing money. Patsy saw Dr. Frisk as a liability to her checking account."

I didn't stick around to hear the rest of what Reba had to say. I knew I had to get to Noah Druck and give him the information I had and free Bernadine.

Chapter Twenty Two

“Where in the hell did they go?” My eyes darted all over the roads as my Beetle sped down the streets of Swanee.

I looked at all the cars I sped past with a little bit of hope that one would be Sean’s truck. I had to get to the police station and let Noah know about the feather.

The idea that Patsy Russell could have killed Henry never even crossed my mind. But the feather was the telltale clue that she was at Henry’s office. Plus the fact that she probably had the crimp tool from my shop. Marlene was going to have to start taking good inventory when we get those bride boxes back. Or I was going to have to change my policy.

But why? Why was Patsy visiting Henry? Was she really after him for a relationship? Why did she do it? None of it made sense. What made sense, was that I had the missing piece to Henry’s murder.

I grabbed my cell out of my pocket and my finger got pricked by the metal piece. I took it out and looked at it. I pulled the car over to the side of the road and took the dental flosses out of my pocket.

I inspected both of them.

Henry's non-wax floss had a metal piece on it but it was different than Dr. Russell's new floss which had two metal teeth sticking up to cut the floss, like the one I found at Bernadine's house.

Why would that have been at Bernadine's?

My phone chirped a text message. I looked at it.

I'm out on bail. Call me. B.

"Bernadine," I gasped and dialed her immediately, putting her on speakerphone.

"It was awful. Just awful." Bernadine sobbed.

I pulled the Beetle back onto the road.

"Lock your doors!" I screamed out. "I need you to call Noah Druck and tell him I'm on my way. I know that Patsy Russell killed Henry. I have the missing evidence to prove it."

"What? What is it?" Bernadine begged to know.

"Tell me one thing." There was no time to answer her questions. "Have you ever had Patsy Russell to your house?"

Somehow I had to put Patsy at Bernadine's to explain the metal floss piece.

"She left a note on my front door that she stopped by to talk about the Barn Dance, but I haven't seen her since. I tried calling her back. Why?" Bernadine asked.

"I don't have time to tell you now. Tell Noah to put an APB out on Sean's truck. Patsy has him hostage." I hung up the phone in hope Bernadine would listen to me and do what I had asked her to do.

When I zoomed past the street where Henry's office was, I noticed Sean's truck was parked out front. I slammed on my brakes and threw the car in reverse. I skidded the car right behind Sean's truck.

Without thinking about my next move, I ran into the office like I was some sort of hero.

"Sean?" I called out into the dead silent office. "Sean?" I asked again, but my voice quivered.

The door slammed behind me. I jumped around. Patsy Russell had a gun in one hand pointed directly at me and her other hand outstretched.

"Give me the feather, Holly." There was a slight twist of her lips. "I won't hurt him if you give me the feather."

I put my hands up and she stuck the gun in my ribs.

"If you don't give me the feather, I will do to you and lover boy what I did to Henry." She pushed the gun deeper into my side, causing me to wince. "Move."

I did exactly what she told me to do as she guided me into Henry's office where she had bound and gagged Sean, who didn't look so big and bad at the moment. In fact, if I weren't in danger, I would have taken great joy in seeing him in the position he was in. Though I would have never wanted him harmed. . .or killed.

"Tell me why you did it?" I asked through the pain.

If she was going to kill me, I at least wanted to know why she caused so much pain. "You are a beautiful woman with so much life ahead of you."

What she had done just didn't add up to me. The whys needed to be answered.

"It's not easy being a doctor's wife. Especially when you have to keep up a good appearance. It costs money." She tilted the gun sideways and had me get back-to-back with Sean.

Out of the corner of my eye, I saw a flash of someone go by the window. I knew Bernadine had called Noah and it had to be the police out there ready to storm the joint and free me.

I didn't resist. I let her tie my hands and body to Sean's. We hadn't been this close since the last time we had made love. Sean's body was tense. I could feel the fear inside of him.

"I deliberately planted the crimp tool just so it would link them to Bernadine. Henry had to go. He was taking all of Kevin's business." She twisted and tied me up. "Kevin said that we were going to have to go on a budget. I wasn't about to let that happen."

Sean's hand grabbed mine and squeezed. Somehow it made me feel better knowing he was there with me. Patiently I waited to see if I could see what Noah and the police force was doing on the outside to free us. I squeezed Sean's hand back.

"I truly went to talk to Henry about the business, but in his smug high-falutin way, he said that it was Bernadine's time to shine after what he had done to her." She had a smug look on her face.

If what she was saying was true, Henry Frisk really did want to get back with Bernadine.

"Everyone in Swanee knows that I'm the best dressed and I wasn't about to let some overweight divorcée come in and steal my thunder." She stood up after she finished tying me up. She haphazardly waved the gun around like it was play pretend. "When he got a little pushy, I pushed back and the next thing I know, I stabbed him with his own knife."

"You are not only beautiful, but you are smart." I coaxed her ego so she would tell me more. "How did you get the knife?"

"Well, I figured he wasn't going to give in so easy and I had already decided that if I needed to kill him so Kevin and I could stay on top, I would. So I paid a visit to Bernadine when I knew you loser Divas were having a meeting and I broke in and took the biggest knife I could find."

That must have been when she dropped the dental floss piece Willow had found, putting her at the scene of the break-in.

"Planting the crimp tool not only placed Bernadine here, the weapon was also hers." She kept the gun pointed at us and tapped her finger. "I'm smart. But dumb at the same time. When I got home, I noticed my feather was missing from my hat. I came back but the police were here. Then I decided to become friends with you by telling my sweet dear hubby that I wanted to learn to bead when in all actuality I already knew how to make those cheap bracelets that you sell at that little shop of yours." A smiled crossed her face. "Honey, do you think I would really want a Holly Harper original when I only shop at Tiffany's?"

The more she talked, the more I wanted to get my bare hands around her perfectly thin neck. I struggled to get up.

"Don't worry. I'm going to go look in that little car of yours for my feather. I'm sure you won't go anywhere." She disappeared out the door.

The sound of footprints got my adrenaline going, but the sound of the gun firing got Sean's going and he was able to free us. We jumped to our feet and Sean tried to hold me back with his arms, but I pushed my way past him and down the hall hoping to see Patsy's diamonds dripping with her own blood.

"Two men coming to your rescue." Patsy pointed the gun at me.

"No!" I screamed when I saw it was Donovan who had gotten shot.

"You don't mess with a Diva's ex-husband!" I screamed with the fire extinguisher over my head.

Her hand was shaking so bad, I knew it was my time to take charge. Without even thinking, I flung the steel cylinder right at her.

A shot rang out as someone flung me to the floor, their body covering mine.

"Police! Police!" I could hear Officer Kiss screaming and footsteps thundering toward us. "We have four people down. We need an ambulance." I heard her call.

Four people? My eyes were closed. I wasn't sure if I had been shot. But I counted out four people. Donovan, Sean, me, and Patsy. *Four down?*

Chapter Twenty Three

"You are one lucky girl," Carol, Dr. Russell's secretary, walked up to the Diva table.

Ginger, Marlene, Agnes, Cheri, Flora, Bernadine and I had decided it was best to go to the dance together. After what had happened with Patsy murdering Henry, we thought it'd be best to stick together like glue as we always had.

"Thanks, Carol." I held up my iced tea.

I wasn't going to argue with her. When Officer Kiss had yelled that four people were down and I counted out the four people and knowing Donovan had been shot, I was lucky. The four of us were sent to the hospital. Luckily, Patsy wasn't good with the handgun so Donovan's thigh was only grazed by the stray bullet and he was treated and released before they let me talk to him.

Sean and I were just checked out to make sure we were okay and not too shaken up. Patsy, I knocked the hell

out of her with the fire extinguisher after she shot Donovan and turned the gun on me.

Sean said that I saved his life. . .again. I told him not to be so flattered.

I tried to see Donovan before I left the hospital, but since I wasn't family, they told me I wasn't allowed to. That didn't stop Diva Cheri who sweet-talked a young orderly into letting her in to see Donovan. Unfortunately, Donovan had just been released and that was how I had found out he had gotten only a surface wound.

Several times throughout the rest of the night and day, I had tried to call and text him with no response. Eventually, his phone went straight to voicemail. He was ignoring me and I was going to have to give him time. Which meant that when the Divas showed up at my post-emergency room bedtime, they talked me into going with them to the Barn Dance.

The entire day, I had fielded calls about the big shoot out and I was sure I was going to be doing a lot of explaining to more as the night grew.

There was a local four-man band that was up on the stage belting out the latest Tim McGraw songs, which sounded a lot like karaoke to me, but who was I to judge? I was just glad to be alive.

The bundled lights seemed to have gotten untangled and strung all over the barn. There were hay bales strewn all around the edges of the barn and were taken up by people's rumps. And the bar-b-que pit was a hit, just like always. But the dessert line, provided by Agnes Pearl and Bernadine's Second Cup, was the hit of the night.

It was true. Bernadine stood to get millions of dollars from the insurance policy that was taken out on Henry and she was planning on donating to a lot of charities, especially the ones that helped children get dental care. It made me proud to see her hard work at Second Cup pay off.

"So you mean to tell me." Agnes Pearl wore a plaid bandana tied around her neck to go with the theme of the barn. She talked with her hands, "Donovan Scott showed up to save you?"

"Yeah." Suddenly I was shocked that he found out that I was there. Even more terrifying realization washed over me when I realized the bullet could have killed him. "Can you believe it?"

I looked out into the crowd and took a big sip of my Mason jar tea. It was sweet tea too. I didn't care about the calories. Life was short and there wasn't going to be a man in my life anytime soon. Willow was enough.

I let out a sigh and looked down at my little piggy, who was fast asleep by my feet.

Cheri reached over and patted me on the back. I didn't dare ask if she had talked to Donovan today. I wasn't prepared to hear the answer.

"How did he know you were there?" Ginger asked a very good question.

For a moment I just stared at her. That was a question I couldn't answer. I looked around the table at my friends, the ones who had never judged my decisions and stopped at Marlene, the least of Donovan's fans.

"Fine." She dug deep in her purse and took out a stick of gum. "He came to the shop saying he was supposed to meet you for dessert at Second Cup. When he was there, Reba came in and wanted to apologize for her behavior." Marlene tipped her cupped hand up to her mouth like she was drinking. "She said that she got nervous when she saw Patsy in the shop while she was there for her bridal appointment. Then she happened to explain what she had heard from Mrs. McGee and how she told you about it at the decorating committee. Donovan asked her all sorts of questions that I didn't understand, then he bolted."

Cheri took a bandana out of her pocket and bent down to tie it around Willow's neck.

"That must have been when he showed up at the barn. I told him you were talking to Charlie and Charlie said that you went to talk to Patsy." Ginger replayed the events of the night in her head. "But I don't know how he got to Henry's office."

"I pinged her phone," Donovan appeared over my shoulder. "I never took the app off my phone and I knew you were in trouble."

I rose from my seat as if propelled by an explosive force and rushed over to his side. I dared not grab him in fear of him rejecting me. But the fact remained that I wanted to. All the Divas had their faces tilted toward him with a look of satisfaction. Even in a crowd, his presence was compelling.

"I . . ." I mumbled like a little baby. Not sure what to say. Not sure where we had left off. "Thank you. I swear I would have met you if. . ."

"She weren't locked in the courthouse with me." Sean walked out of the shadows. "Right, Hol?"

Sean's jaw tensed visibly as he waited for my answer. His lips parted in a display of straight, white teeth. The playboy smile that had made me fall head over heels in love with him. But also the smile that made all the other women fall at his feet.

All at once, the Divas sat comfortably back on the picnic bench to take it all in. There I was stuck in the middle of my present and my past. Only I wasn't sure what the present had to hold. I could look back at my past and knew that it was somewhere I didn't want to travel to.

"Locked. Locked in is right." I moved closer to Donovan and looked deep into his eyes. "I would have come if I wasn't locked in the courthouse after spying on Charlie and Dr. Russell."

It turned out that Dr. Russell was worried the cops would find out that he had stalked Henry's office to see who was doing the decorating. Dr. Russell felt like the finger was pointing to him and the little fight he and Henry had at the committee meeting.

Donovan put his finger up to my mouth. "Shh." His eyebrows rose in amusement. The warmth of his smile echoed in his voice, "You are safe now."

"Thanks for the tip." Officer Kiss walked up to the table, breaking any sort of tension between Sean and me.

Sean seemed to disappear as quickly as he had appeared.

"You are welcome," Bernadine said to Officer Kiss.

"What tip?" I asked and ran my hand down Donovan's arm before our hands clasped between us.

"I told her about how Henry used his phone to dictate," Bernadine said.

That didn't seem like much of a tip.

"We," she pointed to her badge that was neatly pinned on her cop vest, "were looking at phone logs and records. We quickly scanned through his photos, but when Bernadine told us at the station—after we had arrested her—about how he used his phone, I started to look deeper into the photos. That was when I saw a selfie Henry had taken right before his death and in the shadows, I could make out a woman's figure with a hat on." She raised her hands. "Leading me to Patsy Russell."

The band interrupted with their rendition of Eric Clapton's *Wonderful Tonight* and Donovan stepped between me and Officer Kiss.

"I think it's time we show this town who the real man in your life is." He grabbed my hand and took me to the dance floor.

We danced and danced and danced, not a care in the world and let the others fade in the background.

It was the best Barn Dance I had ever been to.

"Would you like a tea to wet your whistle?" Donovan's mouth swooped down to kiss mine.

"Unsweetened, please," I whispered with satisfaction in my soul.

I knew tomorrow I was going to have to meet Bernadine for a few laps around the lake to burn off the sweet tea I had drank. After all, I had a man in my life.

Bride Jewelry Set Holly Harper Style

Necklace, Bracelet and Earrings

Intermediate Level Skills

Bead, Swarovski crystal and gold-plated brass, crystal AB, 6x3.5mm rondelle (49 beads)

Bead, Swarovski crystal, jet, 12x8mm rondelle (26 beads)

Pearl, Swarovski crystal, white, 14mm round with 1.3-1.5mm hole (28 pearls)

Bead cap, gold-finished brass, 6x1mm flower, fits 6-8mm bead (2 bead caps)

Crimp bead, 12Kt gold-filled, 2x2mm smooth tube, 1.1mm inside diameter (4 crimp beads)

Crimp cover, gold-plated brass, 4mm stardust round (4 crimp covers)

Headpin, gold-plated brass, 2-inch, 21 gauge (1 headpin)

Headpin mix, Swarovski crystal rhinestone and silver-plated brass, mixed color, 2.5mm / 3.2mm / 4.2mm round, PP 18 / 24 / 32, 1-1/2 inches, 24 and 21 gauge (2 headpins)

Earwire, gold-plated brass, 17mm flat fishhook with 3mm coil and open loop, 22 gauge (2 earwires)

Clasp, toggle, gold-plated "pewter" (zinc-based alloy), 10mm twisted round (2 clasps)

Clasp, lobster claw, gold-plated brass, 12x7mm (1 clasp)

Clasp, lobster claw, gold-plated brass, 18x6mm flat (1 clasp)

Beading wire, Accu-Flex, clear, 49 strand, 0.019-inch diameter

Pliers, flush-cutter

Pliers, round-nose

Pliers, chain-nose

Pliers, crimping

Necklace:

Step One: Using flush-cutters, cut one 18-inch length of Accu-Flex® professional-quality beading wire.

Step Two: String on to the beading wire one gold-filled 2x2mm crimp bead and the loop on the ring portion of a gold-plated "pewter" toggle clasp. Pass the wire back through the crimp bead, pulling the wire snug against the loop. Place a small amount of adhesive inside the crimp (Loctite® optional). Using the crimping pliers, crimp the crimp bead. Using flush-cutters, trim the excess wire from the short end. Place a gold-plated 4mm crimp cover over the crimp bead then gently close it.

Step Three: String onto the beading wire the following beads:

- One Swarovski white 14mm round pearl
- One gold-plated and Swarovski crystal rondelle
- One Swarovski jet 12mm rondelle
- One gold-plated and Swarovski crystal rondelle

Repeat for a total of sixteen sets, plus one additional Swarovski white 14mm round pearl.

Step Four: Repeat Step 2 to attach the second half of the necklace to the gold-plated 12x7mm lobster claw clasp.

Bracelet:

Step One: Using flush-cutters, cut one 9-inch length of Accu-Flex beading wire.

Step Two: String on to the beading wire one gold-filled 2x2mm crimp and the loop on the ring portion of a gold-plated "pewter" toggle clasp. Pass the wire back through the crimp bead pulling the wire snug against the jumpring. Place a small amount of adhesive inside the crimp (Loctite® optional). Using the crimping pliers, crimp the crimp bead. Using flush-cutters, trim the excess wire from the short end. Place a gold-plated 4mm crimp cover over the crimp bead then gently close it.

Step Three: String onto the beading wire the following beads:

- One Swarovski white 14mm round pearl
- One gold-plated and Swarovski crystal rondelle
- One Swarovski jet 12mm rondelle
- One gold-plated and Swarovski crystal rondelle

Repeat for a total of seven sets, plus one additional Swarovski white 14mm round pearl.

Step Four: Repeat Step 2 to attach the second half of the bracelet to one gold-plated 12x7mm lobster claw clasp.

Step Five: String the following components onto one gold-plated headpin:

- One gold-finished 6mm bead cap
- One Swarovski white 14mm crystal pearl
- One gold-finished and Swarovski crystal 6mm rondelle bead
- One Swarovski jet 12mm rondelle bead
- One gold-finished 6mm bead cap

Step Six: Using round-nose pliers and chain-nose pliers, begin to form a wrapped loop on the straight end of the wire. Prior to making the first loop, pass the wire through the ring portion of the toggle clasp then continue to finish the wrapped loop.

Earrings:

Step One: String the following components onto one silver-plated and Swarovski crystal headpin:

- One Swarovski white 14mm crystal round pearl
- One gold-plated and Swarovski crystal 6mm rondelle bead

One Swarovski jet AB 10mm round bead

Step Two: Using round-nose pliers and chain-nose pliers, form a simple loop on the straight end of the wire.

Open the loop on one gold-plated fishhook earwire and pass it through the simple loop created in Step 1. Close the loop.

Repeat Steps 1 and 2 to create a second earring.

A special thank you to Firemountain Bead Company where I get all my beading necessities. You can find this pattern along with many others on their website.

About The Author

Tonya has written over 15 novels and 4 novellas, all of which have graced numerous bestseller lists including USA Today. Her novels have garnered over ten national awards making her an International Bestseller.

Best known for stories charged with emotion and humor, and filled with flawed characters, her novels have garnered reader praise and glowing critical reviews. She lives with her husband, three teenage boys, two very spoiled schnauzers and one ex-stray cats in Northern Kentucky and grew up in Nicholasville. Now that her boys are teenagers, Tonya writes full time but can be found at all of her guys high school games with a pencil and paper in hand. Come on over and FAN Tonya on Goodreads.

Praise for Tonya Kappes

"Tonya Kappes continues to carve her place in the cozy mystery scene with the witty and endearing *Ghostly Undertaking* set in a small town that is as fun as it is unforgettable."
New York Times bestseller Dianna Love

"Full of wit, humor and colorful characters, Tonya Kappes delivers a fun, fast-paced story that will leave you hooked!"
Bestselling Author, Jane Porter

"Fun, fresh, and flirty, Carpe Bead 'Em is the perfect read on a hot summer day. Tonya Kappes' voice shines in her debut novel." Author Heather Webber

"I loved how Tonya Kappes was able to bring her characters to life." Coffee Table Reviews

"With laugh out loud scenes and can't put it down suspense A Charming Crime is the perfect read for summer you get a little bit of everything but romance." Forgetthehousework blog

Also by Tonya Kappes

Women's Fiction

Carpe Bead 'em

Young Adult Paranormal

Tag You're IT

Olivia Davis Paranormal Mystery Series

Splitsville.com

Color Me Love (novella)

Color Me A Crime

Magical Cures Mystery Series

A Charming Crime

A Charming Cure

A Charming Potion (novella)

A Charming Wish

A Charming Spell

A Charming Magic

Beyond The Grave Series

A Ghostly Undertaking

Grandberry Falls Series

The Ladybug Jinx

Happy New Life

A Superstitious Christmas (novella)

Never Tell Your Dreams

A Divorced Diva Beading Mystery Series

A Bead of Doubt Short Story

Strung Out To Die

Crimped To Death

Small Town Romance Short Story Series

A New Tradition

The Dare Me Date

Bluegrass Romance Series

Grooming Mr. Right

Non-Fiction

The Tricked-Out Toolbox~Promotional and Marketing Tools

Every Writer Needs

Edition: April 2014

Editor: Cyndy Ranzau

Cover Artist: Kim Killion at Hot Damn Design

Made in the USA
Lexington, KY
05 February 2016